BEULAH'S

HOUSE

OF

PRAYER

BEULAH'S HOUSE OF PRAYER

Cynthia A. Graham

Brick Mantel Books
Bloomington, Indiana

Published by Brick Mantel Books, USA

Brick Mantel
BOOKS

www.BrickMantelBooks.com
info@BrickMantelBooks.com

An imprint of Pen & Publish, Inc.
www.PenandPublish.com
Bloomington, Indiana
(314) 827-6567

Print ISBN: **978-1-941799-33-8**
eBook ISBN: **978-1-941799-34-5**

Library of Congress Control Number: **2016937890**

Printed on acid-free paper.

Cover Design: James Graham

For my grandmother, Octavia Prince Odell

Acknowledgments

I would like to thank my mom, Shirley Greenfield, and my mother-in-law, Norma Graham, for advice and lessons learned along the way. Thanks to all those who have encouraged me to keep writing. Lastly, a very special thank you to Jennifer Geist for believing that Barmy, Oklahoma, and all who dwell there, deserved the opportunity to be known. I am truly grateful.

Chapter One

I was born in 1936 on a ragged, wasted little strip of land known as the Oklahoma panhandle. Barmy, Oklahoma, dawdled on the eastern edge of Beaver County, amongst places called Ralph, Hooker, and No Man's Land. They were desperate times and although everyone had been told the only thing they had to fear was fear itself, they knew it wasn't true. There was drought and hunger, insects and sickness, but the most fearsome thing was the dust that would fill the sky and rain down like snow on everything.

Even today, most people don't like to speak directly to the events of that time. To forget, they burned diaries, pictures, and letters reasoning that when you've already lived through hell there could be no need to do it again. But when you're born into times like this, there's a natural curiosity about them and my mama always told me I had more than my share of it.

In her old age, there were days she seemed to be there again. The wind would pick up just so, or the sky would turn a certain shade of green and her eyes would glaze over. Then she'd say, very quietly, "There is another duster coming." Mama always talked in very proper, very precise English. It stood out, oddly, against the drawl of my daddy and the farmers who were our neighbors.

I always longed to know about the days when she and daddy were young, but those times were hard and people must deal with suffering in whatever way they feel is best. Mama's memories were pushed into those unused corners of her mind where they might occasionally break loose in dream, or more often, nightmare, but they were seldom spoken of freely. Still, they lurked there, mixed up and intertwined, like some nasty jumbled spool of thread. When you jerked too impatiently, sometimes the thread would break and she would say, "Well, what would you want to know that for?" But other times, the thread would smoothly untangle and she would tell her story, my story, the one I longed to hear.

It seems my story begins before mama ever knew Barmy, Oklahoma, existed, with the arrival of a woman preacher. They say Beulah Clinton struck a deal with God the day the sky touched the earth and sucked her husband away. Whether she wanted him found dead or alive, no one ever knew for sure, but seeing as they found him dead and she gave her life to God, everyone figured she was happy with the way it turned out.

Beulah arrived in Barmy five days before my mama, during the dog days of August on a wagon pulled by two mules, Eve and Mary; Eve being the naughty one and Mary the good. The town had always been a quiet, self-reliant place, but in 1934, to speak plainly, it was in desperate need of a miracle.

Mr. Jewel Wiley was the first person to speak to her by all accounts. Jewel was one of those thin, wiry men who have a hard time sitting still and an even harder time keeping their mouth shut. He was in front of his drug store, sweeping the sidewalk when, to his surprise, a wagon pulled up.

Jewel had the distinction of having no upper lip, making his teeth protrude from his mouth beaver-like. That fact, added to his round, bulging eyes, always made me think of a squirrel when I saw him.

Beulah halted the wagon and asked in a very thick southern accent, "What be the name of this here town?"

Jewel stopped his sweeping and leaned on the broomstick, looking at the old woman with interest. It wasn't often strangers found their way to Barmy, and it was less often they were old as Beulah. "Ma'am, you're in Barmy, Oklahoma."

"Barmy," Beulah repeated. She looked around her and I reckon no one will ever know what enticed her to stay. It was exactly the same as every other town the railroad laid out along the tracks. There was one stop sign on Main Street at the only four-way intersection, lined by various small shops which were, for the most part, boarded up. There was a gas station at each end of town, the one toward the highway mostly for cars; the other toward the fields mostly for tractors and all around was the flat, dry, dusty Oklahoma panhandle. It was, like many other places at that time, taking the last gasping breaths of the dying . . . its demise expected any day by the people who lived there.

"Can I help you with anything?" Jewel asked her.

Beulah fixed her eye on him and replied, "No, I do the helping. Ya'll got a house of prayer in this town?"

Jewel shook his head. "Last church meeting we had was over a dozen years ago." She said nothing in reply, and to satisfy his curiosity, he couldn't help but ask, "We don't see many people traveling by wagon these days. Ain't you got a car?"

Beulah puckered her wrinkled lips as if she'd just eaten something sour. She leaned her head back and closed one eye as was her habit before she answered, "Cars is the devil's handiwork. They give man too many extra hours and too much time for sin and idle pleasures."

Jewel Wiley had a nice car, so I know he was offended. Nevertheless, he was too fascinated to move. He watched her take her right index finger, insert it into her mouth and hold it up to the sky as if determining the direction of the wind. Then, seemingly satisfied, she nodded and moved on finding a house in the part of town closest to the train tracks, the cemeteries, and the dump.

Jewel, of course, lost no time in telling everybody in town about Beulah. In those days, there were some old-timers who had actually heard of her, although now any knowledge of Beulah Clinton has been relegated to the archivist and librarian. She spent decades ministering at tent revivals and there was talk she had come to pitch her tent in Barmy. When she bought a house and quietly moved into it without a word of revival, the townsfolk concluded that there probably wasn't much left in Barmy to revive anyway.

She moved in next door to my daddy and a more needful place she couldn't have asked for. Mr. Guppy was a drinker and Mrs. Guppy gone. The only child born to them was my daddy, Homer Guppy, and he was as hell bent on hell as any young man who ever breathed in Barmy.

At sixteen, his list of accomplishments was long. In his spare time, he liked to take pot shots at the old empty Barmy schoolhouse. Naturally, the thought of Homer Guppy roaming through town with a gun in his hand was unnerving to most people, so the sheriff intervened and got him to stop. With his rifle confiscated, Homer moved on to arson as a way to pass the time. He also liked to steal cars, knock over mail boxes, and he regularly tortured puppies, kittens, and occasionally small children.

Although people felt most comfortable with Homer when he was at a distance, he really wasn't hated in Barmy. His behavior was attributed mostly to the fact that he had no mother and his father liked to use him for boxing practice.

The first time daddy ever spoke to Beulah she was standing in the yard doing nothing . . . just staring straight ahead. Her yard was a tiny parcel of land surrounded by chicken wire nailed to thick tree limbs. There were a couple of sprigs of grass growing up here and there from the dust and a scrawny cottonwood tree in front near the road. There had probably been a time when the wire was used to keep in chickens, but a chicken must scratch for its dinner and they can't eat dust. All throughout Barmy, these fences were yet another reminder that the land hadn't always hated them and there might come a day when hell would retreat back under the earth's crust.

Beulah's eyes landed on Homer as he walked past her house. Pointing a long gnarled finger in his direction, she said, "You boy. God's got his eye on you."

Homer paused in his steps and stared at Beulah. He looked at her with a blank face; an expression he had learned through closed fisted blows, a way to cheat his daddy out of the satisfaction of seeing pain. But that was part of the mystery of Homer Guppy; no one ever really knew what went on in his mind. When small minded people can't understand you; they tend to decide for themselves just what you are, to help them make sense of things. Most people assumed years back any child of Linford Guppy must be bad and Homer did his level best to prove them right.

Beulah's sudden declaration of God watching him seemed to him a little odd as, to speak plainly, his life wasn't idyllic. A small, seldom-seen crooked smile played upon his lips and before he realized it, he had begun to laugh.

Quickly, Beulah materialized at the fence row. "You think hell a laughing matter, boy? You think it funny to be cast into utter darkness where they is weeping and gnashing their teeth?"

"What are you talking about?"

"I'm talking about you!" she said in an ominous voice. "And the road you're on."

Homer put his hands in his pockets and cocked his head to the side. He was extraordinarily tall and thin and would have been a nice-looking fellow except for the fact that he was frequently bruised, his clothes never fit, his hair was never cut or combed, and he was generally dirty.

"Granny, the only road I'm on is this one right here . . . Grit Avenue."

"Your name Homer Guppy?"

"Yeah."

"Then you're headed for hell just the same as you're headed for town. You got the devil in you."

"There ain't nothing in me," Homer argued. As if to reiterate the point, his stomach growled loudly at that moment.

"There is!" Beulah contradicted vehemently. "When I saw you, I seen Satan hisself, bless God. Once I knew a boy just like you . . . the devil was in him deep. When that demon finally come out it looked like some kind of frog or toad. It went a flying over the house, screaming the whole way and that boy was a fine young man ever since. I'm gonna pray for you. I'm gonna pray every day."

Homer backed away. "Ain't no one ever once said a prayer for me, and I'd take it as a favor if you wouldn't start in with it now."

Beulah simply smiled. Everyone said she had an odd smile, a smile that seemed to penetrate through bone and marrow and into one's soul. "Well," she told him with a soft, kind southern drawl, "we'll just see."

And with that, the doors were opened to Beulah's House of Prayer. The house was always open, which in those days was not so remarkable as no one had anything worth stealing. There was always a pot of coffee on the stove and there was always soup or beans for the downtrodden. People would come in at all hours and Beulah would be on her knees praying, or shuffling through the kitchen, cooking, feeding the hungry, or nursing the sick. No one knew exactly what all she prayed for, but they did know she took plenty of time to pray for Homer, just as threatened. Somehow, a rumor quickly floated through Barmy that she had a stash of money buried in a mason jar somewhere. Many nights would find Homer Guppy lantern in hand, digging hole after hole in the yard when the house was dark and quiet. Most people thought it was a fine thing for him to do as it took his mind off his hell raising.

And so Beulah settled in to do her work and she couldn't have come at a better time. Barmy needed help and there could be no denying that. It was in the midst of the Depression and the cows were bony because grass can't grow in dust. Neither can anything else for that matter. There were no soup kitchens in Barmy, but there was plenty of hunger and desperation and Beulah, for one, liked desperation. She saw it as an invitation.

Chapter Two

If desperation was what Beulah was searching for, she would have been hard pressed to find anyone more desperate than Marigold Lawford. Marigold's memories of the Depression remained vivid and real to her, never locked away like mama's, but all around her, coloring every thought, every decision, every feeling. She simply accepted the Depression, as she accepted everything, with a meek resignation that one might mistake for weakness if one didn't know her. She accepted all of life's malignancy with a manifold grace because her very essence was wrapped up in guaranteeing everything around her remained friendly and peaceable.

Marigold Lawford had been raised on a farm and remembered a time when her family had all they needed—back when she was small. Then came times more lean and finally things got bad enough where they couldn't get any leaner. Her people decided to pick up and join their kin in Napa Valley but their truck was old and they needed a new one. Mr. Ensign Lawford, the richest man in town, offered to purchase them one, and her family had been so grateful they left Marigold behind to become the new Mrs. Lawford. That was in 1931 when she was seventeen and Ensign Lawford fifty-nine. In reality, the whole affair was disgraceful, but Marigold's parents were desperate and

Ensign rich and used to getting what he wanted. Being that he was a strong, virile, and passionate man, his first wife lasted only five years, long enough to bear him one child; a boy, less than a shadow of his father, named Holcombe.

Now, while Ensign was large, powerful and intense, Holcombe was pinched, impotent and greedy: stingy with love, stingy with time, and stingy with money. After Ensign's demise, Marigold didn't understand that, by law, she was entitled to a portion of the Lawford estate and Holcombe didn't bother to explain it to her. He simply made empty promises and put her on the street, unable to even find a piece of bread for her to eat in his rush.

When I was younger, my family lived with Marigold for a time. I always remember her like a billowy fair-weather cloud, soft and unnecessary, but a gentle force that made each day more pleasant. Content to float on the horizon, Marigold never drew attention to herself. As she stood on the street corner, contemplating what it would be like to sleep in the old train depot, a wagon pulled up.

"You need a ride somewhere?" the aged driver asked her.

"No, ma'am," Marigold answered with downcast eyes. She had developed the habit as a child of letting life have its way with her. She never fought for anything, never expected anything . . . thus she never really got anything.

"Train don't stop here."

"I know."

"Bus don't stop neither."

Marigold sighed.

"You got a place to sleep?"

"No."

With that conversation, Marigold Lawford became the first refugee to move into Beulah's house of prayer. It wasn't exactly the kind of place she had grown accustomed to living in, but Marigold never complained. And before that day was over, she would have someone, besides Beulah to keep her company.

The train did stop in Barmy, Oklahoma, on that hot August afternoon for the first time in well over a decade, leaving my mama, one trunk, and a coffin. It was unable to even pull up to the platform because trees had grown between the ties on the spur line, making it hard to drag the coffin across the tracks to the road. The task required five men, and from there the hearse came, leaving mama alone by the roadside.

Sugar Watson, as she was called then, had seen her share of cow towns and this one was a sight worse than what she was used to. She stood at the old broken-down train depot looking tiny and fragile, a small girl, not necessarily short, but slender, like a child. Her face was delicate with high cheekbones and a tiny nose that turned up just enough at the end that it saved her from having a conceited appearance and instead, created an illusion of helplessness. She may have looked young and innocent, but the truth of the matter was, even at fifteen, she was anything but helpless.

"The mortuary is down yonder a ways," a voice at her shoulder told her. She looked up to see Joe Brownfield, the sheriff of Barmy.

Her eyes scanned the expanse of Main Street. The prospect was barren, the stores were mostly empty, and the sun glared down cruelly as if it took great delight in baking the town. A dust devil blew up and spun down Main Street, leaping across the train tracks, flinging tiny pieces of gravel as it went.

This was not what she was accustomed to. She was born and raised in Chicago. Her mother, Marie, had been a trapeze artist and was quite famous in her time. In fact, in 1910, she was featured on a Ringling Brother's circus poster as a famous aerial artist. While Sugar idolized Marie, the same could not be said of her father. He was a sword swallower, or, as she called him, a blade glommer. In reality, his only downfall was in dying during the Depression and not before it like his wife. Sugar was able to connect all of their good times to her mother because Marie had the good fortune to pass away before things got bad.

But things did get bad and Pal found he could not make ends meet working only spring and summer for the circus and began touring with the sideshows that frequented county fairs leaving his impressionable seven-year-old daughter behind with his fair booking agent, Madame Courtier. Sugar got quite an education sitting in that office, a place frequented by the mutilated, the scarred, and the freaks. She scarcely saw her father for eight years. Their trip to Dallas County was going to be their chance to get re-acquainted. Of course, that never happened. He died just outside of town, and as it was hot, and corpses tend to stink, the train stopped at the nearest town. Fanning herself Sugar asked, "What do you call this place?"

Joe Brownfield removed his hat and ran his fingers through his hair, then said in a voice that tried to sound encouraging, "Ma'am, you're in Barmy, Oklahoma, the jewel of Beaver County."

Sugar tapped her foot and looked at Joe. Always impatient and clever, whenever she looked at you in a certain way it was unnerving because she seemed to be able to see inside your skull.

Joe's face flushed red and he quickly mumbled, "Well, maybe it's not really the jewel of Beaver County. We just say that 'cause we're trying to get the state to build a penitentiary here."

To Sugar, the whole place looked like a penitentiary. She made her way to the mortuary and arranged to have her father buried in the free cemetery at the edge of town. Pal Watson should have been buried next to his wife, Marie, in Chicago, but they were out of money and out of luck.

Sugar had one trunk which held her father's swords, her mother's costumes, trapeze rings, two dresses, three pairs of underwear, one winter coat, and two dollars and eighty-seven cents. The trunk was waiting on the sidewalk outside of the mortuary and she sat down on it and put her chin on her hand, taking stock of the situation.

If she could just get back to Madame Courtier in Chicago things would be okay. She liked being with Madame and she liked the fast-paced job of a fair booking agent. The power Madame held in her hands was god-like. Someone would walk into her office and she would look them up and down and pronounce judgment within minutes. To Madame, people were a commodity, the way she made her living, and Sugar had unconsciously picked this notion up. She never looked at anyone without wondering in what way they could best serve her.

Her quick eye assured her nothing in the town of Barmy was of value. The fact that she was stuck there was daunting, but Sugar looked upon it as a challenge, and she loved a challenge.

"You needing help, girl?" a voice asked cutting through her thoughts.

In surprise, she looked up to see an old woman in a wagon being pulled by two mules on the street directly in front of her. It was odd that she could never recall hearing that wagon drive up.

"I am in a bit of a spot," she admitted looking the old woman up and down. She had never seen a human being with as little promise and wondered if there was anything this particular person could do for her.

The woman spoke in a thin, high voice. "My name is Beulah Clinton. I'm a minister of the Gospel." She glanced at the mortuary. "Your folks dead?"

"Yes," Sugar said slowly and suspiciously.

"You got any kin?"

"No. But I sent a telegram to a friend in Chicago and I know she will come for me."

Beulah seemed to be thinking; her head was turned up and one eye was closed. After a moment she said to Sugar, "You can stay at my place until your friend comes. It's just me and Mrs. Lawford so we got the room."

Sugar stood and glanced around her. Another dust devil wound its way through town slowly. She studied Beulah. "Do you have a church?"

"No."

"Then how are you . . ."

Beulah began climbing from the wagon with a little effort. "I go where He sends me."

Sugar looked up and down Main Street. There were only a few stores open, the rest being boarded up. She recalled the two dollars and eighty-seven cents in her trunk and knew that would not keep her in a hotel even if there was one. Making up her mind, she said, "I am obliged to you."

Beulah brushed her aside and picked up the heavy trunk with barely a grunt, tossing it into the back.

As they drove, Sugar announced, "I am Sugar Watson. I come from a circus family. We were on our way to Dallas when daddy . . . well, you know."

"How old are you, girl?"

"Fifteen."

"Can you read?"

"Yes. I can read and figure."

"Do you know anything about the Good Book?"

"I know that at one circus where we worked there was a man named Lenny the Lion Tamer. He did an act where he was Daniel in the lion's den. He would stick his head in their mouths and everything." She was quiet and then added, "Lenny is not here anymore."

"Well, they's a lot more to the Good Book than stories."

"Well, of course I know that, but they do come in very handy. Once I heard of a man who could hold his breath for five minutes. He would dive in a big tank of water and fight with a mighty whale to get him to spit up Jonah. It was really a catfish but no one wants to see someone fight a mighty catfish."

Beulah looked at her out of the sides of her eyes and was quiet so Sugar continued, "I love the circus. Have you ever been? My mother was a trapeze artist, which is what I am going to do. I want to be under the big top not in some lousy sideshow like my daddy. Although, I must admit, the sideshows can be interesting and the people are very nice. The last one daddy was in had Pinhead Pollie, Maybelle the Monkey Girl, Ferdinand the fire eater, Stretch, Chubby, and Bob. Bob eats light bulbs and he can drive a nail into his nose."

"They got any snake handlers?"

"No. Daddy worked at a sideshow once that had a snake charmer, but I have never seen one."

"Gospel of Mark says you'll know God's people because they'll get bit by snakes and not die. Ain't got no snake handlers then they mustn't be God's people. I been bit and I'm still livin'."

Sugar looked at Beulah with newfound interest. "What kind of snake bit you?"

"Snakes," Beulah corrected. "Back in Georgia they'd take whole boxes of 'em and throw 'em up by the pulpit and we'd commence handling 'em and some of us would get bit and some of us didn't. If you died, you died, it was God's timing. I never seen no one die but Mr. Clinton's daddy died that way. But it was his time or he wouldn't have gone."

"You ever think of being in a sideshow Mrs. Clinton?"

Beulah shook her head. "I've got God's work to do, girl. I can't be off working for the circus."

"What kind of work do you do?"

Beulah smiled mysteriously. "Whatever He calls me to."

As they drove through town, Sugar noticed a tall boy walking along the road. Something about him caught her eye and she turned around in the seat and looked at him. His height made him just far enough past typical to be interesting and she noted, with curiosity, that he shook his fist at the wagon.

"Who is the boy that does not like you any?" Sugar asked.

Beulah didn't look back but merely replied, "That's Satan hisself, bless God."

Sugar was interested. "Does he have horns growing out of his head? Once I saw a man in a sideshow that had really honest to goodness horns growing out of his head."

"No, he ain't got horns. He's just ornery."

Sugar was disappointed but looked back again. The boy was still walking, his hands in his pockets, his shoulders slumped, and for some unexplained reason, she liked very much what she saw. He was filthy, his clothes didn't fit, and his hat was pulled down over his eyes, making him look guilty about something. There was no explanation for the interest he created in her, but interested she was. She was attracted to the tall, lanky frame and dark, melancholy face. Perhaps Barmy held a little promise after all.

Chapter Three

My oldest memory is the day my first brother was born. I was over four years old when they finally got around to having another baby. I remember daddy coming into my room in the middle of the night and gently picking me up from bed. He was so young then. His face was thin in the moonlight and his dark hair unruly. Miss Marigold was waiting in the front room and I heard her tell daddy in a quiet voice, "Just go for a drive. Stop and get breakfast somewhere. It's gonna be a while and you don't want that little one hearing anything if it gets bad."

Daddy simply nodded and I remember him lingering at the doorway to the bedroom. The only glimpse I got of mama was a pale, wan smile she gave to us both and then daddy carried me out, bleary eyed, to our old truck. I woke up later with the sun beating down, and noticed how tired daddy looked. His face was covered with stubble, his eyes red and sleepy. He smiled when he saw I was awake and said, "Today, we're having donuts and Coke for breakfast. But don't tell your mama." It was the start of a camaraderie that would last a lifetime.

We arrived home to the news that daddy had a son. Marigold had to go home and take care of her own family and I remember daddy hesitating at the doorway and mama calling him in. I stood in the hallway, remembering the closeness I had felt to him and wanting it back. It hurt to be alone, outside of the circle of love on the bedstead in their room. Mama looked up and saw me. "Come see your baby brother, sweetie." I will never forget how it felt to be welcomed, how it felt to be loved.

Mama's first memory of Barmy did not leave that sort of impression. She did not feel welcomed when she arrived at Beulah's house of prayer. In fact, any feeling of hopefulness quickly disintegrated. Beulah Clinton lived in a shotgun shack. It was a poorly made little shanty, with one large room that served as kitchen, dining room, and sitting room and three small closet-like rooms that were bedrooms. There was no electricity or running water, the cooking and heat both came from a stove that would burn wood, coal, and if necessary, cow chips.

Sugar crossed the threshold and took off her gloves, surveying the scene with dismay. Unexpectedly, one of the doors opened and a young woman appeared. She was beautiful, everything about her was plump and sensual, reminding Sugar of the girls that Madame routinely sent to work in "cooch" shows. And, yet, for all this voluptuousness, she had the smile of an innocent child.

"Well, hello," she said in a light voice.

Sugar could tell the dress she was wearing was very elegant even under the large white apron that she had covered it with. She offered a stark contrast to the makeshift home in which she was living.

"Hello," Sugar replied, trying to fathom where this person could have come from and what connection she could possibly have with Beulah Clinton.

At that moment, Beulah entered carrying Sugar's trunk. "I put those vegetables in the soup, Miz Clinton, just like you said. Is there anything else I can do?" the young woman asked.

Beulah paused and said kindly, "No, child."

"Mrs. Clinton, I could have gotten that," Sugar told her, embarrassed that the elderly woman was carrying her trunk.

"No matter," replied Beulah. "I see you and Mrs. Lawford have met." She said it more as statement than question and then quickly left to put the two mules in their little shed in the yard.

The woman came forward with her hand out. "I am Mrs. Marigold Lawford," she said emphasizing the missus. To Sugar, the handshake seemed trepidatious and weak. It did not leave a good impression.

Sugar was trying to determine what the young woman's place in the house was. She appeared to be a maid; she was stirring a pot of soup on the stove and sweeping the floor. But that didn't seem to make sense to Sugar. Marigold was dressed in very fine clothing while Beulah was wearing a dress of homespun cloth.

"I am Sugar Watson." She paused a little uncertainly and asked, "Do you work for Mrs. Clinton?"

"No. My husband just died and I got no place else to stay. Mrs. Clinton took me in until I can go home." This was spoken as if there were nothing odd in it.

Sugar stared and then asked, "Go home? What do you mean?"

Marigold sat down on a chair and folded her hands in her lap. This was a gesture she had acquired as a girl, a quiet surrender, a telltale meekness that caused people to take advantage of her. "I mean when my stepson, Holcombe, lets me come home."

"I don't understand," Sugar told her shaking her head in confusion. "Why would you have to leave?"

Marigold explained the particulars of her marriage to Sugar with no emotion. This was her reality, there was no shame. She had spent four years with Ensign Lawford, four years of being pampered and loved and used, and in her own vacuous way, she came to love and depend upon him. It had been a devastating blow when she awoke to find her husband dead next to her in bed. She pulled her handkerchief out of her pocket, wiped her eyes with it, and then twirled a piece of embroidery thread that had come loose from it around her finger.

"And he didn't have a will?"

"I thought he did," Marigold said with her eyes wide and believing. "Holcombe says he can't find it. Now, it's just a matter of finding the marriage license. I remember Ensign putting it in the safe, but Holcombe says it's gone. He's looking for a copy of it at the courthouse."

"So you let an old man use you for four years and you have nothing to show for it?"

Marigold pursed her lips and knitted her brows. "I don't know what you mean by being used. He was my husband."

"Then why are you here?"

"Holcombe says it would be 'unseemly' if we stayed in the house together."

"Then why did he not go?"

Marigold appeared confused.

Sugar was trying to understand, but found that she was growing annoyed. "So he sent you here to live with Mrs. Clinton?"

"Not exactly. Mrs. Clinton found me on the street."

"He put you out on the street?"

Marigold nodded and Sugar felt the anger in her rise. She didn't understand how anyone could be so weak, but she didn't understand Marigold. Marigold accepted Holcombe's decision because it was simply her nature. To argue or fight with Holcombe would have never crossed her mind.

"Did it ever occur to you that you could have refused to leave the house?" Sugar asked in amazement.

"No," Marigold answered with downcast eyes.

Sugar rose abruptly and began pulling her trunk to her room, afraid she would say something rude to the simple-minded girl. Immediately, Marigold was there to help her and it was a good thing. Beulah might have been able to wield the heavy trunk, but it took both of the other women to get it to Sugar's room.

The day was long and tiresome. Marigold found plenty to do in the house, cooking and cleaning, and Beulah was always moving, praying with those wayward souls that wandered in, and nursing the sick. Sugar, on the other hand, had never been left to her own devices and did not know how to fill her time. She watched Marigold and Beulah hard at work and if the thought to pitch in and help ever crossed her mind, she didn't acknowledge it to anyone.

She plopped on the porch and put her chin on her hand. Her eyes took in the stark landscape. It was barren, dry, and dusty; there was little color and no beauty. Beulah's yard was pitted with holes and trenches as if an angry mole tore it up for meanness and moved on. Once, she called in to Marigold and asked, "How long do you think it takes for a telegram to Chicago to be answered?"

"I'm sure I don't know," was the predictable answer.

The day might have been long, but the night was an ordeal. After midnight, the need to use the outhouse arose and Sugar couldn't resist no matter how hard she tried to think of something else. The idea of being out in the darkness was not appealing; Sugar never liked the dark, and the lantern was not hanging in its usual place.

Glancing outside, she saw that Marigold already had it, and was making her way back across the yard. Sugar waited on the porch and Marigold was almost there when she stumbled in one of the holes. From the darkness, a hand appeared. It picked up the lantern and shone it in Marigold's face.

"You ain't Miz Clinton," a voice said. Suddenly a hand grasped Marigold's wrist tightly and pulled her roughly to her feet. Sugar saw the voice belonged to the tall boy who was walking down the road.

"I'm Marigold," she said in a meek voice. Then she cried out, "Ow! You're hurting me." Sugar looked around wondering what she should do, knowing she couldn't fight with the boy. She spied an axe and had just picked it up when she heard him say, "If you're looking for the money, it's mine."

"Money?" Marigold repeated. "I don't know what you mean."

His clasp became tighter. "Don't fool with me."

"I'm not! I live here . . . for now."

He let go of her wrist and she began to rub it. Sugar put the axe down and leaned forward, listening to the conversation with interest.

"You live here?" the boy repeated. "With the witch?"

"She's not a witch. She's just a very old woman."

"You know where she keeps her money?"

"What?"

"Her money," he repeated. "I hear tell she's got a Mason jar full of it. I need it a heap worse than she does."

"What for?"

His eyes drooped. "I don't know exactly. Just to get away."

"From Barmy?"

"No," he answered uncertainly. "Just my dad."

"Did he do that to you, dear?" Marigold asked gently indicating a swollen nose and bloody lip on the boy's face.

He appeared to be startled by the word "dear." His face changed at once from the menacing snarl to an oddly wistful boyish face.

"Don't see that it's any of your business, but yeah, he done it. He does it all the time."

Marigold reached out her hand to touch the boy's face, but he immediately backed away. "So, why are you here? You kin to Miz Clinton?"

"No, I'm just staying here 'cause I got no place else to go. My husband died and I'm trying to figure out what to do."

He paused in his searching and looked her up and down. "If that Mason jar's as full as everyone says it is there'd be enough in it for both of us. You living in the house . . . you might be able to find something out." He looked at her questioningly.

She hesitated and finally said, "I'm sorry, but I ain't a thief. Leastways, I could never steal from someone who went out of her way to help me. I could never steal from Beulah."

He shone the lantern in her face and studied her. "You ain't another holy roller like her are you?"

"I ain't been to church in years, so I reckon not. My husband wasn't much of a God-fearing man. He always said God was for the weak and helpless but he was neither so he didn't cotton much to Him."

"I ain't weak or helpless neither," the boy said proudly as the blood trickled from his nose. He put the lantern in her face again. "I know you. You're Marigold Starling, ain't you?"

"I'm now Mrs. Marigold Lawford," she replied with the emphasis on the *missus*.

"That ain't what I hear in town."

Marigold's face grew white and she put her hand over her chest. "What do you mean?"

"I hear tell that you and ol' man Lawford weren't never married. They says you was what they call a mistress."

Marigold gasped. "I weren't nothing of the sort! I was his bona fide wife. Why are they saying that?"

He shrugged. "Don't know. People say things in front of me 'cause they don't notice I'm around."

Marigold's face wore a puzzled look. "It must be a mistake."

"You sure you was married?"

Marigold's eyes opened wide with indignation. "Of course, I'm sure. I ain't no fornicator. Holcombe Lawford will set everyone straight. He knows we was married, he was there."

"Anyone else there?" the boy asked.

"Just my mama. She's in California now."

"Well, then, I wish you luck." He swung a shovel over his shoulder, and started walking slowly toward his home.

Sugar hid as Marigold went back inside, still rubbing her wrist, and then she leaned over the porch railing, watching the boy as he made his way next door. Marigold might not be able to steal from someone who had gone out of her way to help her out, but Sugar had no such scruples. The boy was young, strong, and fierce and Sugar knew he could come in handy. He could be very useful, indeed.

Chapter Four

When I was about eight years old my daddy went to war. During this time, I became fascinated with calendars, counting the days he had been gone, the number of days until his tour of duty would be over, the amount of time that had elapsed since I last saw him. We had gone to live with Marigold for those two years. Daddy didn't want us alone and Marigold was mama's best friend. Looking back, it was probably a horrible imposition, mama and her four children moving in, but I never once remember hearing Marigold complain.

One Sunday afternoon I had my calendar pages spread over the floor the way I always did. I remember distinctly asking mama, "How long does it take to make a baby?"

She had been putting away dishes and she paused saying, "Nine months, generally. Why?"

I spread my calendar pages neatly on the table. "If you and daddy got married in May and I was born in January that is only eight months."

Mama closed the cabinet door and sat down in front of the table looking at the evidence I was presenting. "Yes, it certainly seems that way," she finally said, quietly.

I plopped in the chair beside her and put my chin in my hand and stared at the calendar pages with her. "How do you suppose that happened?" I asked, innocently.

The question made mama smile and I was glad. She rarely smiled while daddy was gone and I had missed seeing her happy. Impulsively, I climbed into her lap and took her face in my two hands, kissing her tiny nose. "Well?" I asked.

She put her forehead against mine and said, "It happened because your daddy taught me how to love and because he saved me from leaving Barmy." It would be another eight years before I finally understood what any of that meant.

In 1934, leaving Barmy was the only thing mama had on her mind. She was always looking east, down the railroad tracks, wondering how she could get back to a place she understood, a place she could recognize. To be honest, mama really wasn't exactly sure where Barmy was, but she knew it wasn't on any map she'd ever seen.

Her first order of business was to bury her daddy. My grandpa, Pal Watson, was planted in the best free cemetery Barmy had to offer. With him being a stranger in town, there was a good-sized crowd for the burying. Everyone crowded around the coffin and looked to Beulah to do the preaching.

My mama could have right then and there earned a reputation for being a hard-hearted little thing. She was never one prone to tears. In fact, I only recall seeing her cry one time in my whole life, that being on the day daddy left home in his clean, pressed uniform. Luckily, her light blue eyes were so unused to the harsh glare of the Oklahoma sun that by the time the funeral rolled around they were red, swollen, and watering.

"The poor little orphan," murmured someone in the crowd. It was acknowledged by everyone in town that it was good

Beulah had taken her in as not many in Barmy could have fed another mouth.

Beulah stood over the gaping hole carved out of the dust and began, her thin, high-pitched voice rolled over the prairie gathering everyone's attention. "Pal Watson was a man who met his maker unexpectedly. No man knows the hour when the Lord will come a' knocking, so we must always be ready."

"Amen," said most of the crowd. Barmy, Oklahoma, hadn't entertained anything like a church service in a dozen years. It wasn't that the people of Barmy didn't believe in God, there was just the general feeling that He had forgotten them.

"Barmy, Oklahoma, is a town flooded with sin, sin against the weak and the old. God don't like that none." Then, her voice raised and the crowd looked on expectantly. They knew she was a Holy Ghost preacher and were hoping for some kind of rolling on the ground or speaking in tongues. "But Pal Watson ain't here amongst that anymore. He's in a place where the streets is paved with gold." She raised her hands and said in a loud voice, "And God shall wipe away all tears from their eyes and there shall be no more death. Neither sorrow nor crying and no more pain."

"Amen," responded the hopeful townsfolk.

"Hallelujah!" Beulah proclaimed, beginning to bounce. "The angels is rejoicing over Pal Watson tonight." The crowd waited, holding its breath and hoping for something out of the ordinary to occur.

It did when Sugar tugged on Beulah's sleeve and whispered, "He was an atheist."

The raptured look Beulah's face had been wearing departed. "What did you say, girl?"

"I said he was an atheist."

Beulah was unfazed. "Ain't no man an atheist when he feels the cold, tight fist of death on him. Mark my words, you'll see your daddy again one day in heaven."

Sugar didn't really care much about it one way or the other. Her selfishness had been ingrained sitting in the office of Madame Courtier. It had taken root the day Wee Walter, the Midwest's smallest man, had pinched her rear and said she showed promise and had sprouted the day Doris, the fat woman, yelled at her. She remembered sitting on the floor of Madame's office listening as Doris was being interviewed. In her memory, she could hear the fat woman's labored breathing; she had been fascinated with her chins, watching them wobble as she spoke. As she stared, Doris fixed an angry eye upon her and shouted.

Sugar didn't remember exactly what she said, but she remembered the horrible tight feeling in her chest, as if Doris had raised herself up from the chair and had crossed the room and struck her. She looked to Madame to protect her and she waited to hear what she would say. For the rest of her life, she was able to recall plainly the hurt she felt when Madame ignored the outburst and continued with her interview as if nothing had happened. At that precise moment in time, mama realized that she must always take care of herself because no one else on earth would. Madame wouldn't, and her father had become like someone that came by once a year to sell seeds or encyclopedias. It was odd, the feeling she had as she left the cemetery. She didn't feel sad, because Pal was dead, she felt sad because, to her, he had never really been alive.

As they left, most people said they enjoyed the sermon, though none of them knew Pal. Normally, after a burying there would be a lunch, but since there wasn't a church in town and Pal had no family there, people were in a quandary as to what should be done. In the end, Sheriff Brownfield offered to buy everyone an ice cream cone at the drugstore, and that's what they did.

Jewel Wiley opened the place, and the town streamed inside. It was small, and there weren't many seats, but people didn't seem to want to sit anyway. They liked to be crowded up at the soda fountain where they could catch up on the gossip and laugh at their troubles.

Jewel quickly got behind the soda fountain, put on his white apron and began serving up cones. His bald head was beaded with sweat as he made one after another. It was probably more ice cream than had been served in that store in years. He gratefully sat down when he served the last cone to Sheriff Brownfield.

As soon as he was sure everyone was treated, the sheriff made his way for the door. Although kind-hearted and generous, Joe Brownfield was naturally shy. He was a young man with skin that was always burned red from the sun and dark eyes that were generally shaded by his hat. There was nothing remarkable about Joe, his height was not tall or short, his build not slight or hefty. He was one of those people everyone liked when he was around but no one remembered when he wasn't.

He was to the door, with his hand on it, when he was distracted from leaving by the presence of Marigold, sitting quietly alone at a table trying to fade into the ether.

Before he knew what he was doing, he found himself sitting across from her. He simply sat there, looking down at his hands and not able to find his voice.

After a few moments, Marigold said to him, "Your cone is melting, Sheriff."

He looked down and noticed that the ice cream was beginning to run down the side of the cone. He smiled, abashed, and quickly licked it off his hand. "It was a nice funeral service, wasn't it?"

"First preaching I heard in years."

"Miz Clinton did a right nice job, too," Joe remarked.

After a pause, Marigold told him, "It was kind of you to treat everyone like this. I know it must mean a lot to Sugar."

They both glanced over at her. She was up at the counter talking to some young people and they were all laughing. "She seems to be taking it real hard," Marigold added simply because it seemed to be the right thing to say.

Again, they sat in silence, eating their ice cream. Occasionally, their eyes would meet and they would smile. They said very little, but seemed to enjoy the evening.

After the ice cream, Beulah, Sugar, and Marigold walked home. "Do you like that sheriff you were sitting with?" Sugar asked Marigold with interest. To be truthful, she didn't care for Marigold when they first met. She was about as interesting to talk to as a wall or maybe a table leg, appearing to be a milksop, the kind of girl Madame would hire as maid and then roundly abuse, getting some sort of perverted pleasure from seeing tears form in downcast eyes.

Marigold had been smiling a little to herself, but it quickly faded. "Why, I'm a widow. My husband ain't been dead a month yet. I couldn't possibly."

Sugar opened the gate for the others. "I heard someone say that Mr. Lawford was not your husband. They say that you were scammed."

Marigold put her hand over her heart and stopped walking. "But it ain't true! We was married. I can't understand why everyone is talking like that."

Beulah turned to Marigold. "The Lord says it's easier for a camel to go through the eye of a needle than for a rich man to see heaven."

Beulah and Sugar kept walking and Marigold stood in the yard, probably wondering what needles and camels had to do with lying townsfolk.

As they entered the shack Sugar asked Beulah, "Have you ever seen a dromedary camel? I rode one at a circus once in Milwaukee."

Chapter Five

In September of 1944, we received a letter from the United States Government informing us that daddy was missing in action. For twenty-three days I pored over my calendars, marking each day with a thick black "X" and waiting each morning at the post office in town for a letter. Mr. Wiley would often give me a cinnamon stick as I waited there and sometimes he even gave me a Coke. He would talk about what he had heard around town, trying to take my mind off things, but his voice would trail off when the mail truck appeared. Each day I would run in, and invariably, I would come out, my face long and my shoulders slumped. He always sent candy home for my brothers and Marigold's children.

Late in the month a letter arrived and my heart jumped. It was daddy's handwriting. I ran out and triumphantly showed Mr. Wiley the envelope and he sent home a quart of ice cream. Mama's hands shook as she opened the letter, and no matter how hard she tried to read aloud, her voice would not work. She quickly scanned it and finally said, "Your daddy is found. He is in a hospital in Belgium and will be fine." Even before this episode, though, mama had always hated September. She said it was because the month made her apprehensive; everything that wasn't dying was reduced to scrambling to survive the winter.

She always said the September when daddy was missing was the worst one of her life and I know that was true. But, the next worse had to be her first one in Barmy.

Though the Depression was hard on everyone, it seemed to take out most of its rage on a tiny strip of land known as the Oklahoma panhandle. Being there, to mama, was a profound punishment. She was even deprived of the familiar cycle of seasons and soon learned nothing was more depressing than Barmy in autumn. There was no Indian summer, no assault of color, no comforting smell of leaves burning. The air got cooler, the cottonwood leaves paler and one morning they had all tumbled to the ground and it was cold.

She plopped on the porch unhappily and put her chin on her hand. As Marigold walked by her she couldn't help but ask, "Why does anyone live here on purpose?"

"They don't," Marigold replied creeping to the outhouse to throw up again. It seems Ensign Lawford had left her with a parting gift, and it was beginning to show.

Mama would be the first to admit that she hated everything about Barmy when she first got there. Her eyes watered constantly from the harshness of the sun, the dryness of the air made her lips crack and her nose bleed; the drought caused spiders and centipedes to turn up in her bed at night. Besides the harshness of the land, the people were of a sort she had never encountered before. Nothing was done quickly or with purpose. They had no ambition, no plan. They simply lived day to day, hand to mouth. Even the way they talked was hateful to her, bringing to mind the stinging smack she received upon her cheek at ten years of age from Madame when she accidentally spoke the word "ain't."

Madame had lifted her chin and looked down her nose at mama and said, "In my presence you will speak proper English only. People will not respect you if you use slang. Your yes will be yes, your no will be no and you will not use contractions. Is that understood?" Not only was it understood, it was fixed permanently in her mind, a sort of dogma that remained her entire life. The slurred, drawled dialect made mama cringe. She prayed she would receive a letter from Madame soon . . . she wasn't sure how long she could endure the ignorance.

Once again, she studied the odd maze of holes and tunnels in Beulah's yard. She had waited for the boy the night before but he had never shown up. Trying to get some information, she remarked, "Mrs. Clinton, you have something tearing your ground to pieces."

Beulah looked at the holes and simply replied, "The only thing tearing up my ground is Satan hisself, bless God. It's just dirt and it keeps his mind on something besides his troubles."

"Who is Satan, and why is he digging in the yard?"

"He's the boy over yonder," Beulah replied. "I reckon it's the devil makes him dig 'cause that's who I see when I look at his face."

Sugar confronted Marigold and asked her the same question, not entirely satisfied with the answer she got from Beulah.

"It's just Homer Guppy, the boy next door. He's convinced there's money buried somewhere in this yard, but I reckon if Beulah had any money she wouldn't be living here. Leastways I know I wouldn't."

Marigold might not have believed there was money somewhere on the property, but Sugar was convinced of it. There was always food; someone was always knocking on the door looking for help. Beulah had the label of kind-hearted woman, even if she did make you listen to a sermon and pray with her to get a bowl of soup. In the past week, Sugar had seen Beulah feed and give money to a rag man, a hobo, and a veteran of the Great War.

Her mind had already begun to work and she could never shut it down once it grabbed onto an idea. If she found that money she could get back to Chicago, back to Madame Courtier and the agency. She could walk to the next town, plop the money on the counter and buy her own train ticket. Wouldn't Madame be surprised to see her walking through the door of the agency? Sugar would just look down her nose, the way Madame looked at her and say, "Well, Dear. I certainly could not wait for you to take the situation in hand, now could I?" Her telegram had still not been answered, and truthfully, she wasn't sure it would be. She hadn't finished her trapeze training. It all hinged on how much promise Madame thought she showed and Madame was so conservative with her praise, Sugar had not the least notion of her own worth.

Never mind the fact that Beulah fed her three square meals a day and gave her a roof over her head. Sugar needed that money and had no qualms about taking it. Homer Guppy had been thorough, yet there were still plenty of places to dig. Nothing Sugar could think of was more distasteful than digging in the dirt, but she remembered, with pleasure, the skinny boy stalking down the road and decided it was time to put him to use. She waited for him at the fence row and he finally came into view.

"Hello, Homer Guppy," she called over to him as he walked down the road in front of the house.

He stopped seemingly confused. "Hey," he returned. It was pretty obvious by his blank stare that he did not trust her.

Sugar studied him and determined right away he was just what she needed. His face was hardened and ruthless, the kind of ruthlessness borne from desperation. It seems odd, but when she looked at that face, she found something in it that was appealing. His eyes were dark and sleepy. They seemed to be lazy, but when you looked closer you could see a sort of starvation, a need to be touched. His mouth was thin, hard and set, as if not accustomed to softness or smiling. With her quick eye, she noted the bruises on his face. "You been in a fight?"

"No. My dad just give me a thrashing, that's all."

"What did you do?"

"Looked at him wrong."

"You looked at him wrong?"

He simply nodded.

"Well, where have you been?"

Homer shrugged. "Just to town."

Sugar came closer and leaned her elbows on the fence post, a piece of grass sticking out of her mouth. "Is there anything to do in that town?"

"Not really."

"Then why go?"

Homer's eyes went uneasily toward his house. "Gets me out of the house, that's all."

"My name is Sugar."

"I know. I heard about you in town."

"What did you hear?"

"That your dad died on the train, and you're stuck here like the rest of us."

"Well, I might be stuck here, but I am not like the rest of you."

"What do you mean?"

"I mean if I can get away from here, I can get a job, a way to make a living. Have you ever been to the circus Homer Guppy?"

"No."

47

A quick idea came to her mind. She loved performing more than anything on earth, and Homer looked like a ready audience. "Would you like to see my act?" she asked him with a hint of excitement in her voice.

"Your act?"

The color in her cheeks heightened. "I am a trapeze artist. You ever heard of that?"

Homer nodded.

She glanced around. "Can you climb that tree and hook a ring to it?"

"Yeah."

"Wait here." Sugar ran into the house and returned with the ring she used to practice with. She let him in the gate and instructed him, "Put it on of those lower branches. It is a puny little tree, and if the branch breaks, I would not like to fall far."

He meekly did what he was told. Homer Guppy had never been meek a day in his life, but Sugar talked so fast that he didn't have time to think of a reason to argue with her, and she was so beautiful that he wasn't sure he wanted to. He had always been avoided by girls; the reasoning of all the fathers in Barmy was if your last name was Guppy, no good could come from you. The fact that he stole a car a couple of times a month probably didn't help his cause much with the paternal element in town either.

Sugar wasn't from Barmy and she didn't have a father to worry over her now. She needed Homer's help and she did not hesitate to use the tools at her disposal, these being bright eyes and full, red lips. They seemed to do the trick because evidently Homer was confounded by the deep blue glance that kept trying to catch his eye, and the sweet smile that was foreign to anything he was used to.

He jumped from the tree and dusted his hands when he was finished. "Now what?"

"Wait here. I have to put on my costume." She scampered inside. To her, there were few things in life more satisfying than performing for an audience, even if it was a non-paying, dirty teenage boy. Homer waited and was rewarded minutes later by seeing her come out, scantily clad in one of her mother's circus costumes. To most people, she might have looked a little comical. The costume was too big, and wasn't the tight, sexy ensemble it had been on Marie Watson. It was raspberry-colored satin, cut very low in the front and very high on the thigh. A gold braid followed beneath where Sugar's breasts should have been, but Sugar was not endowed like her mother, so it lay in the middle of her stomach.

She may not have been plump and voluptuous like Marie, but everything she had was tight, firm, and peeking out, and it is safe to say that Homer had never been subjected to so much feminine flesh at one time. His eyes never strayed as Sugar climbed the tree and the next thing he knew she was hanging there from the leather ring by her teeth, dangling before his eyes like some sort of forbidden fruit.

As she hung there, a group of onlookers began to form, but he was unaware of them, his eyes were so full of bare white skin. Sugar began to spin in the air, her arms out to her sides, and the crowd began to applaud in appreciation.

She finished her act and shimmied back up the rope. A couple of people pitched pennies in her direction before they left, and Homer quickly scooped them up.

She went back to him, breathless and smiling, and he handed her the pennies. His face had changed from one of callous indifference to one of blatant admiration. "What did you think about that?" she asked proud of the performance she had just put on.

Poor Homer stuttered and stammered and finally blurted out, "I gotta go." He ran home leaving her half-naked and confused standing at the fence row.

Chapter Six

Daddy came back from the war when I was about ten years old. I remember lying in my bed at night and it always seemed that right after I had gone to sleep, he would start screaming. It scared me and I would lay in my room with my heart pounding, the covers over my head, and listen until mama could get him to stop. I could hear her voice, speaking gently to him, telling him he was safe, telling him he was home. The screaming would cease and then, I would steal into their room and lay down on the floor. It always took a long time for me to get back to sleep after that. Daddy's breathing would be normal, but I knew mama was awake. Sometimes, I think he never woke up at all; he never seemed to remember anything in the morning. But I did, and so did mama.

At that time, her fear of the dark came back. She had an old painting of the Virgin Mary that she placed on her dresser. In front of it she burned a menagerie of colored candles. Their flickering was calming, the light they threw upon the wall just bright enough to chase away the shadows and make me feel safe.

They seemed to have a calming effect on daddy, too. His nightmares gradually faded away, but mama still kept those candles burning. They were there to comfort her and to illuminate that picture, a reminder that miracles are not always what we expect them to be.

I always thought it odd that mama had that picture. She was not Catholic. In fact, the family of Dewey Lee Cope were the only Catholics of which Barmy could ever boast. Dewey arrived with Ensign Lawford in the spring of 1890, when they were both eighteen and Beaver County was called Seventh County. Dewey was always known as Ensign's man . . . detail oriented and loyal. His loyalty was never doubted; he had named each of his six sons Ensign. There was Ensign Columbus, Ensign Franklin, Ensign Valentine, Ensign Rudolph, Ensign Grover Cleveland and then, because his imagination was wearing thin, there was Ensign Ensign.

Dewey would have been the kind of man mama hated if she had met him in Chicago. He was loud and boisterous; he cracked his knuckles, chewed tobacco and cursed. For some reason, meeting him in Barmy made him acceptable to her, probably because the plains were big and the people needed to be too.

Marigold was sitting in a chair with her hands folded in her lap when a loud step sounded on the porch and the door opened in a forceful way that caused the hinges to cry out in protest.

"Mrs. Lawford," Dewey said in a gruff voice. "What the hell you been doing with yourself?"

A bright smile covered Marigold's face. She and Dewey were close. He had taken her under his wing as she had tried to navigate the maze that was her life with Ensign Lawford.

"Why, Mr. Cope," she said mildly. "What a surprise."

He crossed the room and sat before her, his boots thumping heavily on the floor. "I hear you and Mr. Lawford have made a little one," he said in a surprisingly gentle voice.

"Yes," she replied with a faint blush. Then, as if remembering her manners, she said, "This is Sugar Watson. Sugar, this is Mr. Cope."

Sugar wiped her hands on the apron provided for her by Beulah and then held out her hand. "Pleased to meet you, sir."

Dewey rose and removed his hat, revealing a thick head of white hair. They shook hands and he said approvingly, "A nice sturdy handshake, young lady."

Sugar said nothing but studied him with interest. Dewey sat back down and told Marigold, "I wanted to make sure you was okay. Miss Beulah treating you right?"

"Oh, yes. She is very kind."

"This thing with Holcombe, it might take a little longer than we expected. You gonna be okay for now?"

Marigold nodded and Dewey looked like he wanted to tell her something. Evidently, he decided against it as he turned his attention to Sugar.

"Young lady, how are you liking Barmy?"

"Aside from being treated like a slave, I am managing." One of the first things that Beulah made clear to Sugar was that room and board would be earned. Unlike Madame who did no cooking, Beulah's stove burned non-stop. She was always in the process of making soup or baking bread and Sugar was expected, as was Marigold, to make sure the stove was always lit, the soup was not scalding, and the bread was never burned. These chores were things Madame would have hired out, and Sugar inwardly seethed at being asked to do such menial work.

"Where you from?" Dewey asked her with a friendly twinkle in his eye.

"Chicago," she replied with dignity.

"Now there's a cow town for you."

Sugar was appalled. "Cow town? Why she has opera houses, museums. I do not know what you mean by cow town."

Dewey brushed her aside. "Now don't be getting your bloomers in a knot. She is a cow town, the best slaughter houses in the world are there. I should know . . . I was born in Chicago."

"You come from Chicago, also?"

"Yeah. Ain't set foot in it in nigh on fifty years. Left it at fourteen, right after the Haymarket riots. You might have seen her opera houses and museums, but all I ever saw was the bloody floor of the slaughter house. I met up with Ensign Lawford in Kansas City and we finally found our way out here, and I never missed Chicago."

"Never missed Chicago?"

"A man can breathe in Oklahoma. I can stretch out as far as I like and never see another soul. Never missed a thing about the city." He hesitated for a minute but then added, "I do miss my church. Out here, my communion is the wheat I grow and the blood I sweat."

"Never missed the city?" Sugar repeated unable to get past that part of the conversation.

He grinned at her. "I reckon you're in a hurry to get back?"

"I would give anything to get back to Chicago." She frowned and added, "But I have nothing to give. I suppose it would take a miracle."

"A miracle you say?" He reached up to his neck and was removing a chain just as Beulah entered the room.

"Good day, Mr. Cope," she said to him.

"How do you do, Miss Beulah?"

"Lord's seen fit to show me another day." Pausing she asked, "You take Holcombe Lawford to the courthouse today?"

Dewey's opinion of Beulah Clinton was and remains to this day that there was something a bit other worldly about her. He could never get past the notion that she knew things impossible to know. "Yes, ma'am."

"Mr. Lawford see the judge?"

"Don't rightly know," he answered mildly. "He asked me to wait outside."

"I reckon he did."

A knock sounded on the door and Sugar rose to let the sheriff in. Joe Brownfield entered the house and removed his hat. He was a man who never moved quickly, never got in a hurry about anything. He stood there hat in hand for a moment and then, running the brim through his fingers said to Beulah, "Ma'am, Holcombe Lawford came by to see me and filed a complaint against you."

Beulah sat down heavily in her chair. "Did he now?"

"Can you tell me what happened?"

Beulah smoothed her hair back from her eyes with a gnarled arthritic hand. "Why, Sheriff, you know how I am once I get to sermonizing."

"He says you threatened to kill him."

Beulah cackled.

"I gather then that this is just a misunderstanding?"

"Sheriff, I only went to him to ask him where he'd been. He weren't in no mood to answer my silly questions. I told him the Good Book says things done in shadows will be brought to light. He ain't interested in the Good Book and was glad to say so."

"Is he well?" Marigold asked.

"He was a bit worked up by the time I left him. Other than that, I think he was feeling just fine, child."

Dewey cracked his knuckles gleefully. "What else you tell him, Miss Beulah?"

"Oh, just how shadows is funny 'cause they seems so safe, and yet, any shifting of the light and they're gone, what's left behind is naked to the world."

"How did he take that?" Dewey asked.

"I reckon not too good."

"I don't understand how he could have taken that as a threat." Joe said.

"Well, I did mention to him what the Bible says about the widders and orphans. About how the Old Testament says if you raise a hand to a widder or orphan and they cries out to God, he's gonna hear 'em. I just mentioned to him that the Bible says if you hurt a child it's better to have a millstone around your neck. He didn't much like it when I explained him all about millstones . . . about how they is used to grind things."

"I still don't see how he might have taken that as a threat."

Beulah smiled a little when she said, "Then I looked at him real close like, Sheriff. You know how I do." She leaned her head back and closed one eye. Joe nodded and she continued, "He seemed nervous, like he'd been up to something. I asked him if he'd ever been ground by something. He wanted to know if I was threatening him, but I told him that it was God who does the grinding."

"I see. So that was Holcombe's threat." Joe crossed the room and gazed down at Beulah with his honest eyes. "Mrs. Clinton, I suggest you steer clear of Holcombe Lawford. He's as spiteful as they come and if you make too much trouble for him he'll have the state troopers come for you."

"When they arrested Peter the cell doors just swung open. I ain't afraid of Holcombe Lawford, Sheriff; man can't do nothing to me." She looked into his face. "You shouldn't be afraid of him neither."

"Oh, I'm not afraid." Joe assured her. "Just cautious. You should be, too."

Dewey, nodded in agreement. "He's a slippery one, Miss Beulah, and his only interest is himself and his own comfort."

Beulah shook her head. "Holcombe Lawford don't bother me none. It's those he is trying to hurt that is my concern."

"The poor dear," Marigold said sadly, shaking her head. "Is he as bad as all that?"

Sugar rolled her eyes in exasperation.

Joe looked at Marigold the way a parent looks when they explain there is no Santa. "He can be where his money is concerned. But, don't you worry about it none."

Dewey agreed. "You just worry about that little one you're carrying. Holcombe's a grown man. He can take care of himself."

Marigold looked troubled. She pulled on her bottom lip and vacantly stared ahead of her, but said nothing more.

Joe put his hat back onto his head and said, "Well, I reckon I should be going. I'll tell Holcombe I spoke with you."

Beulah nodded and Marigold crossed the room. "I'll show you out, Sheriff." They left the house together slowly, as if trying to stretch a short amount of time.

Dewey grabbed his hat and said, "I guess I should be going, also." Nodding to Beulah he said, "Good seeing you again, ma'am." He turned to Sugar and then remembered something in his hand. Handing it to her he said, "You said you needed a miracle and this is what they call a miraculous medal. My wife likes me to wear it, but I think you need it more."

Sugar took it in her hand and studied it. "Why miraculous? Is it magic?"

Dewey smiled. "No. I always looked at it as a lucky charm, but the missus says it's a prayer. I reckon you can decide for yourself what it is. You said you needed a miracle, and maybe it will bring you one."

Sugar looked at it and squinted one eye. "She's pretty. Is it Mary?"

"Yep. The Blessed Mother herself. They say she was about your age when she gave birth to Jesus."

"My mother's name was Mary. When she became an aerial artist, she changed it to Marie . . . she said it sounded more exotic." She looked at the medal another minute and then put it around her neck. "Thank you, Mr. Cope."

After he was gone, Beulah asked her, "You Roman Catholic?"

"No."

"Then why you need an idolatrous medal of Mary?"

Sugar looked at the medal. "Because it reminds me of my mother. There is something very appealing about her face. It is very kind and gentle. In a way, she looks like Marigold."

Beulah didn't look at the medal, declaring it to be a graven image. But she did look at Sugar oddly when she said, "Be careful when you start asking God for miracles, girl. Sometimes you get them." Glancing in the stove, she told Sugar, "Need more wood, girl."

Sugar took one last look at the medal and then, unhappily, went to the woodpile on the back porch to bring more in.

Chapter Seven

After daddy got back from the war, he went to work in town at Nichols' garage. He had always wanted to work on cars and the army had taught him how. One day, I was in their bedroom looking for scraps of material to make doll clothes when I came across an old cigar box. I opened it and saw a group of beautiful shiny pins and ran with it to mama.

We sat down at the table and looked at the pins together and she reverently lifted each one out of the box patiently explaining to me what they were. "These are your daddy's medals from the war. This is for good conduct; this is the Victory Medal. This is his Bronze Star and his Combat Infantry Badge. This is the Silver Star." Her eyes rested on the last medal, the one I thought was prettiest.

I lifted it from the box and asked her, "Is that George Washington?"

She took the medal from my hands and laid it lovingly in her palm. I was surprised to see her eyes fill with tears. "Yes, that is George Washington. This is your daddy's Purple Heart. He got it at the hospital in Belgium."

The medals were so pretty and shiny that I asked, "Why doesn't he ever wear them?"

She smiled. "Where would he wear them to?"

"Church?" I ventured.

Mama painstakingly laid each medal back in its box and closed the lid firmly. "He does not want to wear them, honey. He wants to forget them."

No one could have foreseen such heroism from him when he was younger. I have observed that every town has at least one person that no good is expected from. Sometimes it's a hermit, sometimes it's a drunk, other times it's a womanizer, but they're usually ignored, mostly avoided, and generally underestimated. Barmy had daddy, the son of the town drunk, a boy who mischief followed like dust after a good hard wind.

Arson was one of his specialties. Any time a farmer found a haystack burned he figured it was Homer Guppy. Any fire at the side of the highway, burnt shack, or brush fire was attributed to him. Some were his work; others were the work of sparks by the train tracks or stray lightning, but Homer got blamed just the same.

October had come around and the nights were cool and crisp. Sugar was still waiting to hear from Madame Courtier and she wanted to find Beulah's money. Her first experiment with Homer Guppy had been a failure. He seemed to be avoiding her now and she desperately wanted to make him a proposition.

She was impatient, her mind always working, and she lay awake at night trying to figure out ways to speak with Homer. But sometimes we don't have to plan; sometimes opportunities fall in our laps. She was disturbed from her thinking one night by the sounds of shouting and people running up the road, and she hurried to the front door.

"Quick! Bring water," came a shout.

"What's going on?" a voice asked.

"Damned Homer set fire to the feed store. He'll go to jail this time for sure."

Sugar stepped out onto the porch dismayed. With Homer gone her chances of finding Beulah's money would be diminished. She sat down and put her chin on her hand and shook her head.

A shadow creeping through the yard caught her eye and she knew immediately by its height that it was Homer Guppy.

She hesitated a moment. It was dark, and the moon gave very little light. She could never shake the feeling that something was hiding in that blackness, unseen and hateful. Madame always made her take out the trash from their apartment and sometimes it was done at night. Sugar would creep down the stairs and then quickly run outside to the trash barrel and run back in as fast as she could. There was always the feeling that something was chasing her, something that wanted to swallow her alive. She would compose herself before going back into the apartment. Madame hated any kind of weakness. She had done a good job of covering her fear, Madame never knew it existed, but it was a heavy, suffocating feeling.

She took a deep breath and then slipped over, whispering, "Homer?"

He peeked out from behind a shed and saw her. "What?"

"Why did you burn the feed store?"

He looked disgusted. "I didn't burn the feed store. I'm not that stupid, but they'll put me in jail anyway and I didn't do it."

"Where have you been?"

"Out walking. I stay out till my dad goes to sleep. I was just walking home when I heard the commotion. They're all saying it was me." He kicked at the dirt unhappily. "It really don't matter, I was bound to end up in jail sooner or later anyway."

Sugar's eyes landed on the pump outside the kitchen and she suddenly had an idea. She tore the bottom of her gown off and ran to the pump wetting it, then returned to Homer.

"Kneel down and be still," she instructed him putting her hands on his shoulders and pushing him to his knees. She began to wash his face, scrubbing with little tenderness and lots of elbow grease.

He pushed her back. "What are you doing?"

"Cleaning you up. Now hold still!"

She continued until a handsome tanned face emerged from the filth. She caught his eyes and said, "Homer, you are right smart looking when you are clean."

"Shut up."

"I mean it. Now come on," she said taking his hand and leading him to the porch.

"What are you doing?" he asked drawing back. "You want me to get arrested?"

"Trust me."

He hung back for a moment and then finally decided, "I reckon I'm going to jail anyway so I might as well get it over with."

She led him to the front porch and they sat on the edge together watching the commotion. A man running by with a bucket of water happened to glance over and paused in his steps when he saw Homer. He ran off at a faster pace and Sugar told Homer, "Sheriff will be here in a few minutes. Follow my lead."

As expected, Sheriff Brownfield arrived. He walked up, put his foot on the porch, and looked down at Homer and Sugar. "Homer, where you been tonight?"

"Out walking, Sheriff. Like every night."

"You been to the feed store?"

"We went another way," Sugar interjected quickly.

Joe looked surprised. "You been with Homer all night?"

"Yes, Sheriff."

"In your nightgown?"

"Yes. I have to sneak out to see him."

"Why would you sneak out to see Homer?" Joe asked obviously confused.

Sugar nuzzled Homer and kissed his shoulder. "Just because."

"Yeah," Homer said in a loud, bold voice. "Because."

Joe was shocked. His eyes were wide and his mouth hung open slightly. "So you're saying you didn't set fire to the feed store?"

Homer shook his head and put his arm around Sugar tightly. "I been busy."

Joe pushed his hat back and ran his hand over his forehead. "Alright, Homer. Glad to hear it." He paused. "You been in school this year?"

"Ain't going no more."

Joe shook his head. "Homer, I've told you time and again, you could make something of yourself if you . . ."

Homer rose. "Sheriff, I know it. I've heard it. Can I go now?"

Joe sighed. "Yeah, you've got an alibi."

Homer and Sugar rose from the porch and walked away slowly.

As they left, Marigold's light voice could be heard calling the sheriff from the doorway. It troubled Sugar. Marigold knew she hadn't been with Homer all night. As they walked away from the house, Sugar couldn't help but wonder if she would tell.

Homer's hand was rough and large, it clumsily held onto hers until the sheriff was out of sight, then he promptly let go.

They had returned to the shed where she had found him. "Why'd you do that?" he demanded.

"Because I need your help."

"What do you want?"

She caught his eyes and held them, replying meaningfully, "I want the money, just like you do."

He tried to pretend stupidity. "What money?"

"The money you are digging in this yard to find."

He said nothing.

"If we work together we might be able to find it," she offered.

"Maybe."

"You sure it is here?"

Homer just shrugged. "Can't think of any place else it could be." He looked at her curiously. "Can you?"

"Not now. I will put my mind to it and see if I think of something." She paused and then held out her hand. "Partners?"

He nodded and took the small hand offered to him. "You got a good, firm handshake for a woman," he remarked to her.

"A person judges you by things like a handshake," she replied repeating something Madame had taught her years ago.

He didn't let go of her hand right away and she wasn't quick to draw it back. It was human contact, comforting in the darkness. "What will you do with your share of the money if we find it?" he asked her.

"I need to get back to Chicago."

"You got kin in Chicago?"

"No," she replied evenly. "I have no kin." She tried to sound steely, giving her best imitation of Madame Courtier, but at fifteen, she had not been as practiced in covering up her feelings. Even Homer had to notice the blinking of the eyes and the uncomfortable shifting of her feet. She quickly turned her face away from him. He seemed to be seeing more than she was accustomed to. Fixing her face in her most business-like expression, she said, "Meet me here tomorrow night after the lights are out in the house and we will get to work. Deal?"

He nodded. He let go of her hand and she was alone again. She wanted the feeling of touch again; she didn't want him to leave so soon. "You ever kiss a girl before Homer? You know, on the lips."

He smirked. "Girls are afraid of me."

"Not me." She moved closer to him but he backed away. "Where are you going?"

"I best get home."

"Why?"

"It's late."

She looked up into his face and smiled invitingly. He seemed confused, but unable to resist that face for long began to lean toward her. At that moment, Sugar made a surprising discovery. She wanted Homer to kiss her. She could feel the want rising up from her belly and landing in her chest with a thump, forcefully, taking away her breath. It made her uncomfortable, so uncomfortable, in fact, that as his face reached hers, at the moment she could feel his breath on her cheek, she pushed him back with all the force she could muster.

"What do you think you are doing?" she asked.

"I thought you wanted me to kiss you."

"Maybe, I do," she replied sweetly. "But not tonight. After we find the money. Okay?"

He looked disappointed. "Okay."

"Tomorrow night, then?"

"Tomorrow night," he grumbled back. He started for home and then paused. Turning back he said, "By the way, thanks for the help with the sheriff."

"Anytime."

That night, Sugar lay awake bothered by what had taken place. "What has gotten into me?" she wondered. She needed Homer's help to find the money and that was all. She had to remember that. She was acting stupidly. A figure at the doorway startled her and she sat up quickly in bed. It was Marigold.

"Sugar, why did you tell the sheriff you were with Homer all night? You were here."

"Did you set him straight?" Sugar asked her voice cold with disdain.

Marigold's mouth formed into a little pout. "Of course not. But why on earth would you lie to the sheriff about Homer Guppy?"

"He needed my help, that is all."

"Why'd you want to help him?"

She shrugged. "Just because."

Marigold looked unconvinced. "Sugar, don't hurt him. You don't know about him, about how hard his life is. If you break his heart, I'm afraid he'd do something desperate."

"What makes you think I would hurt him?"

"Will you?"

Sugar was surprised by such a blunt question from Marigold. So surprised, she had no ready answer.

"You're not staying here in Barmy, and he's got no place else to go."

Sugar plumped her pillow roughly in annoyance and turned away. "Homer does not need you mothering him. He can take care of himself."

Marigold said nothing, and yet, she wouldn't leave.

"What?" Sugar said in annoyance.

Marigold crept into the room and sat at the end of the bed. "What do you think of the sheriff?"

"Why?"

Marigold began to chew on her thumbnail. "I don't know. It's just . . . he wanted to know if he could check in on me now and then. Do you think that would be a good idea?"

"Do you want him to check in on you?"

The chewing of the thumbnail stopped and Marigold's brows knitted together. "Yes, I think I do."

"Then, it is a good idea. What are you so worried about?"

"I just hate people talking about me, that's all. Seems like this will just give 'em all more to say."

"He is the sheriff. People look up to him. You do not have to worry about it."

Marigold rose slowly. "Thank you, Sugar," she said from the doorway. She hesitated there a moment and said, "And Homer?"

Sugar turned back toward the wall roughly. "It will be fine, Marigold. Please, just go back to bed."

Marigold obediently did as she was told, but she and Sugar both lay awake that night while Homer snored happily next door.

Chapter Eight

The night sky in Oklahoma is a vast and wondrous thing. The moon rises brilliantly, setting fire to the horizon and accusing you of being small and insignificant. I remember as a child lying on the grass outside with my daddy. We would stretch out lengthwise, the crowns of our heads touching, and he would point out the Big Dipper, Hercules, Aquarius. I loved being out there with him. He smelled of sweat and tobacco and Old Spice, comforting smells that even now conjure images of beautiful summer nights. I never tried to count the stars as a child, they were simply my friends and I needed no inventory. I reveled in them, in the constellations my daddy showed me, in the filmy grace of the Milky Way.

My mama missed all of that her first autumn in Barmy. Instead of the sky, her eyes were trained on the end of a shovel, watching it bite into the dust. Night after night she met daddy and night after night they dug, searching for a Mason jar full of dreams. She held the lantern as he worked, muscles straining, sweat staining his white shirt, waiting to see if on this night the dust would produce anything of value.

To daddy, it was a labor of love. It was the first time in his life someone was waiting for him, the first time anyone seemed to care whether he was dead or alive. He looked forward to seeing mama all day. Mama was fond of daddy, too, more so than she would have let on.

She worried over him more than she would have liked, too. She didn't like that he was bruised so often, she didn't like that he was neglected, and she didn't like that he was so thin.

"Does your father ever feed you?" she asked him one night critically surveying the thin boy in the loose, awkward shirt.

Homer threw the shovel down disgusted. It was evident the hole he was working on would produce no miracle this night. Shrugging, he replied, "Most of the money goes to Saucy Martin, daddy's bootlegger. There usually ain't much left for victuals."

They sat down together on the porch. "How do you eat?"

"Saucy usually leaves me some canned beans and a little cornbread and soda crackers. Once I was so hungry I ate a grasshopper."

"You did not."

"Sure, I did."

"Did you eat its eyes and everything?"

Homer laughed. "Naw, I pinched his head off."

"What did it taste like?"

"Don't know. I swallowed the bugger whole."

Sugar scooted a little closer to him. She liked him close. When he was there the darkness didn't seem as suffocating, the town didn't seem so all alone on the vast Oklahoma Plain.

"Homer, you ever thought about leaving Oklahoma? Have you ever wanted to go someplace else?"

"Don't know where else I'd go."

Sugar looked around her, at the pale darkness that was illuminated by the moon and the stars. "There are so many other places. It is so . . . dark here." She said it weakly and felt foolish.

He smiled. Sugar liked his smile because it was shy and crooked; it produced a dimple on one thin cheek and made him look like a little boy.

"You afraid of the dark?" he asked in surprise. "I didn't think you were afraid of anything."

Sugar would never admit fear to anyone. The truth of the matter was, growing up Madame Courtier's favorite method of punishment consisted of putting her into a small, dark closet and locking the door. Whether this was what caused her to be afraid of the dark, she couldn't say, but it probably didn't help.

Rather than admit to Homer a weakness like fear, she simply argued, "I am not afraid of the dark. But this town is so small and alone. It feels like a good wind would scour us all off the map and no one would ever remember us."

"No one would ever remember Barmy and that's a fact," Homer agreed. "Ain't much here you'd call 'memorable.'"

"Then why stay?"

"Cause I know Barmy. I know what the sky looks like at night and I know what the wind feels like during the day. I know from what direction a storm could blow up, where to look for the blanketflowers in July, where to find shade in the heat of the day."

Sugar looked doubtful. "But it is so flat and dull."

"Oh, it ain't flat. Tomorrow when the sun's up, look again. It's flat, but sloping, always climbing toward the sunset like it's swollen, like it's in agony, rising toward something it ain't ever gonna reach."

"You like it here," Sugar exclaimed in surprise.

"No," he answered. "Like I said, I know it." They were silent a minute and then he told her, "Sheriff came by the house today."

"Why?"

"Wanted to make sure my dad hadn't killed me. He said he ain't heard one complaint about me in two weeks and he was worried."

"That sheriff likes you," Sugar remarked.

Homer shrugged. "Don't know why." But Sugar knew. There was more to Homer than what met the eye. He looked like a useless bum, a castoff, but there was something in his soul that was captivating.

"Homer Guppy," she told him, "I heard from someone in town that once you tried to shoot a teacher."

"Ain't true. I was shooting at a bird on top of the school-house and I missed, that's all."

"They say you almost took his mustache off."

Homer smiled but said nothing.

"What makes you so bad?"

"I ain't bad," he protested. "Just bored. Besides iffen I were so bad would you be sitting here with me?"

"Maybe," she replied. "Maybe I like bad boys."

Homer shook his head. "That's stupid. Of course you don't like bad boys, and you know I ain't bad. Half the stuff they say about me ain't true and neither is the other half."

"I hear you set a cat on fire."

"Ain't true. I set a barn on fire and the cat was inside. Wouldn't have burned the place if I'd known it was in there."

"I hear you drove Miss Pet Henson's car into the river."

"Didn't mean to. I was gonna bring it back when I was through with it."

"I hear you soaped Mr. Jewel Wiley's shop windows."

Homer smiled sheepishly. "I did do that. What are you checking up on me for anyways?"

"Because I want to know how bad you really are. I need to know if I can trust you."

"Well, what do you think?"

Sugar screwed up her face and studied him. "I am not sure."

He shook his head. "Of course, you can trust me. We're friends ain't we?"

Sugar had never had a friend. His usage of the word almost startled her. Madame had colleagues and clients, partners and confederates. But she never had friends and neither did Sugar. It was a cozy, intimate little word; it conjured visions of laughter and secrets, but she wasn't sure she liked it. The word brought to mind thoughts of openness and sharing, obligations and caring for someone else. Sugar had never known love or friendship, only self-interest and narcissism. The benign monosyllabic word was surprisingly frightening.

"Sure, Homer," she replied because it was what needed to be said. "We are friends."

"Then, you can trust me. I'd never do anything to hurt you."

"I believe you," she told him.

He didn't ask her if she'd ever do anything to hurt him. Perhaps, he really didn't want to know the answer.

Chapter Nine

Growing up, daddy was my best friend. While I loved mama, there always seemed to be a part of her she simply would not let me see. She had an unfathomable beauty, almost like the stars that daddy and I studied. I never got tired of looking, but there was always something there I couldn't quite grasp, something I couldn't get my arms around.

I know daddy felt that way about her, too. Sometimes I would watch him when he came home from work. He would pause in the doorway and mama would be in the house cooking dinner, on the porch doing the laundry, or taking care of one of my little brothers. There was tenderness in her eyes and around her mouth that was wholly beautiful and he would gaze at her, with his head cocked to the side, as if he didn't quite understand how she got there, how this woman could be in his house. He knew it was never her intention to stay in Barmy, Oklahoma.

She kept him working at night trying to find the money to leave, and sometimes she kept him working during the day. She had quickly discovered that the most distasteful chores assigned to her by Beulah were things Homer would gladly do in exchange for a crust of bread and a bowl of soup. Beulah left every morning to visit the sick and homebound and as soon as she was gone, Homer would sneak over. He cut firewood, he cleaned the little shed where Eve and Mary slept, and he even washed clothes. The thought that she might be taking advantage of the hungry boy never once crossed Sugar's selfish mind.

But Sugar didn't stay idle while Homer did her chores. By the time November rolled around, she had investigated most of Beulah's house. She had searched through the pantries, the storm cellar, even Beulah's dresser drawers had been laid bare to her eyes. Every search came up empty, every day brought more frustration because she knew somewhere in that house was her means of escape.

She had checked under the floorboards of her room and now, she knew she must check Marigold's. Walking through the house, she noted no one was inside. She stole into Marigold's room, silently, knowing it was wrong, but feeling no guilt or shame. These were feelings she had long ago learned had no advantage, useless emotions that she had become accustomed to ignoring.

Once inside, she began the wearisome task of knocking on each and every floorboard in the room, listening for something different, for a hollow sound, anything that would make that place stand out. She had scarcely begun when she heard a voice at the doorway.

"Sugar? Is there something I can help you with?"

Sugar looked up to see Marigold. Abruptly standing, she said, "No. I just . . . came in here to look at this picture and noticed something on my foot. I was brushing it off." She crossed the room to Marigold's nightstand. Picking up the picture, she sat on the bed and asked, "Is this Mr. Lawford?"

Marigold came inside and sat beside Sugar looking at the picture. "Yes, that is Ensign."

"He was a handsome man," Sugar remarked honestly. He was wearing a rich business suit with his hat pulled down cockily over one eye. There was a cigar in his hand, and evidently, he had been laughing when the picture was taken. He seemed an odd match for Marigold. He looked worldly and shrewd, like the businessmen in Chicago that would march past the men asking if they could spare a dime, past the children selling apples, past the new mothers begging for milk money. Marigold wouldn't even kill a spider unless it was a black widow. How odd their life must have been together.

Marigold looked at the picture like someone looks at a portrait of George Washington, recognizing the quality of the subject, but having no real connection.

"Did you love him?" Sugar couldn't help but ask.

Marigold's brows went up and her face wore a puzzled frown. "He was my husband."

Sugar shook her head. "That is not what I asked. Did you love him?"

"Yes," Marigold replied with certainty.

"Why?"

At first, Marigold seemed to not understand the question. Finally, she told Sugar, "I loved him because I had to. It would have made our lives together very disagreeable if I had not."

"So you forced yourself to love him?"

"No. I chose to love him."

Sugar shook her head. "It all seems a little silly to me. Love this and love that. What is the real value in it, anyway? Really, what is the point?"

"Why would you think like that?" Marigold asked.

"Because I know what love does to a woman. I know the limitations it places upon her. In 1910, my mama worked for

77

Ringling Brothers. Madame always said she was as good as La Bella Carmen or any of the other aerial artists that they head-lined. She would have been world famous except she met my daddy and married. Madame says it was the biggest mistake of mama's life. She was never as graceful and agile because from then on she was distracted. She was constantly torn in two, trying to please my daddy and herself. Madame told me to always remember, you cannot soar if your heart is grounded on earth."

"But your heart can soar," Marigold said with a smile playing around the corners of her full lips.

Sugar rolled her eyes. "The only soaring I intend on doing is in the big top. Do you know all the circuses have three rings now? That means they will need more performers than ever."

Marigold pulled at her bottom lip and said quietly, "Sugar, it seems so sad and lonely to be up there away from everyone. Is it?"

Sugar rose to leave. "Perhaps. But I have never minded being alone."

"I hate it," Marigold said with a pout.

Sugar paused in the doorway. "I am sure that the sheriff would be happy to keep you company any time."

She was satisfied to see Marigold blush faintly and she went back to her own room, closing the door. She leaned against the door with her back and Marigold would have been surprised to see the one tear that insisted on sliding down Sugar's cheek no matter how hard she tried to stop it.

Beulah was still gone when an old car came to a halt in front of the house, coughing and sputtering. Sugar was sitting on the porch and watched curiously as an elderly man opened the door with some effort and then, wearily, climbed out, stretching and looking around him.

He saw Sugar and began slowly making his way toward her. He was small and very dark; his head and hands seemed enormous in contrast to his withered slight body.

He paused before her and asked, "Is this the place they call the house of prayer?"

"Yes," Sugar replied in a nervous voice. It wasn't that she was afraid of the elderly man; she was afraid he would ask her to pray with him. It was enough that Beulah forced her to bow her head at every meal, she would not bow her head with every strange person that roamed into town.

The man removed his brown hat and rubbed his bald head with his hand. "I hear I might get a meal here. Ain't et in a couple of days."

Sugar felt somewhat relieved and she rose from the porch. "Follow me."

They stepped in the house and Sugar's eyes quickly scanned the room for any sign of Marigold. Unhappily, she noted Marigold was not inside which meant she would have to serve the food.

"Please, sit down," she told him brusquely while she went to the pantry and got a bowl. As quickly as she could, she put the food in front him knowing the sooner he ate the sooner he would be gone.

The man ravenously tore at the piece of bread and devoured it rapidly. Then, with the edge taken off his hunger, he began to sip the soup as if it were a luxury, slowly savoring every bite. His eyes went up to Sugar and he said, "I'm grateful to you. It ain't easy to find a meal these days."

Sugar noted that his large hands were spattered with paint. "Do you paint for a living?" she asked trying to make conversation.

"I am an artist."

"An artist? How on earth did you find yourself out here?"

"Just passin' through," he told her taking another spoonful of soup. "My name is Jeff Walkingstick. Been on the road for about three weeks now. Come from Poinsett County, down in Arkansas and am making my way out west, to San Francisco."

"San Francisco," Sugar repeated dreamily. "I have always longed to see San Francisco."

"She ain't quite what she was before the earthquake, but they're working at it. I'm planning on opening a studio there. Used to be, I could sell my pictures and that would pay my way cross country. Most people ain't got money for pictures these days, though."

"Where all have you been?"

"I've been all over this land . . . from Maine to Washington, from Florida to California."

"Well, you certainly would not want to find yourself stuck here in Oklahoma."

He shrugged. "It's the same as every other place I've seen."

"I do not see how that can be. There is nothing here. It is a tiny blot on the landscape."

He took a sip of coffee and sniffed then told her, "When you get to be my age you realize, it's the people that make the place . . . not the other way around. People here in Oklahoma are just the same as they are everywhere else in the nation. They want a nice place to live and breathe and raise their families. No matter what any politicians in Washington say, they ain't second rate and they ain't stupid. They just want to make a living and keep their families comfortable."

"And that is it?" Sugar asked in surprise. "That is what it is all about?"

"That's all that matters."

Marigold entered the house at that moment. "Hello," she said in her cheerful, light voice.

"This is Jeff Walkingstick," Sugar told her. "He has stopped for a meal."

"I am Mrs. Marigold Lawford," she told him with the emphasis on the missus.

"Married, are you?" the man asked.

Marigold's face fell, just a little. "I am a widow," she told him her hands covering her stomach protectively.

His eyes noticed it and he nodded understandingly. "Marriage is one convention I could never have any part of."

"Why is that?" Marigold asked him.

"Because I am an artist. Wouldn't be fair to marry a woman because I would always be looking at her with an eye to perfection. Ain't nobody perfect."

He rose from the table and stretched again. "I'm mighty obliged to you for the meal," he told Sugar. "Why don't you two ladies come out to my car and I'll give you a picture in exchange for the vittles. And don't tell me no. Nothing worse than not being able to give your art away."

The women followed him out to his car. It was filthy and dust covered, the tires were bald, and it smelled like it had been burning oil for a very long time. He threw open the trunk revealing various paintings of different sizes, all depicting the curious combination of either Jesus Christ or clowns.

"Take one you like," Jeff told them with pride.

Sugar's eyes immediately fell on a picture of a clown. He was standing in the big top and just to the right of his shoulder was a flying trapeze, upon which an aerial artist was sailing. Sugar's lips parted slightly, ready to snap the picture up when, out of the corner of her eye, she noted Marigold looking longingly at a portrait of Jesus holding a small, white lamb.

Sighing, Sugar said, "Could we have the Jesus picture?"

Jeff slammed the trunk closed and got into his car. "Thanks for the food and conversation. This is a nice town, here. Good people. Maybe I'll see you again someday."

Sugar was thinking, "Not if I can help it," as the car drove away.

Chapter Ten

Growing up, my little brothers always thought Christmas was the best day of the year. I, on the other hand, always preferred Thanksgiving. Every year mama and I would get up early and go over to Miss Marigold's to help cook the meal. Then, at about noon, daddy and my brothers would show up.

I always remember Marigold as being pregnant on Thanksgiving, and she probably was. She ended up having nine children in all. After we ate, the men and boys would all go out in the yard and play football and we women cleaned up. For some reason, it never seemed like an unpleasant task on Thanksgiving. There was plenty of food and good company and mama and Marigold would laugh together, recalling stories of their children. After dessert, the grownups would all play pitch and I would watch, not understanding the card game, but enjoying the laughter. It was a far cry from that first Depression-era Thanksgiving mama spent in Oklahoma.

Thanksgiving fell on the twenty-ninth of November in 1934. It made for a lean Christmas as businesses complained there weren't enough days for folks to shop. FDR might have paid attention, but in Barmy it didn't seem to matter. There was no money to buy anything regardless of which day Thanksgiving decided to show up. The president said in his proclamation that we had turned our minds to more spiritual things. Beulah may have been interested in the spiritual, but most people's minds were on things more tangible.

There were few turkeys in Barmy that year and they were quickly bought up by Holcombe Lawford though no one could figure who he was going to feed with them. In the end, most people made do with a chicken and some canned green beans.

Sugar noted, with interest, that Beulah arrived home with a chicken, some sweet potatoes, and pecans for a pie. There was never a lack of money and Beulah did not receive mail; no checks, no government assistance came in. She simply always had just what was needed.

"That Homer is getting lazy," Sugar thought to herself unhappily. They spent every night out in the yard when everyone was sleeping, but soon the ground would be too cold to dig. They'd work tonight, holiday or not.

She was anxious to have the money. She had finally received a reply to the telegram she sent Madame Courtier. Madame would not be west until April, and even then, could make no promises as to whether or not she could get the train to stop. To Sugar, this translated to, at least six more months in Barmy with, perhaps, no end in sight. She absolutely rebelled against this notion. If Madame wouldn't come for her, she'd go to Madame.

She half-heartedly basted the chicken when told but was really little help to Beulah and Marigold in the kitchen.

"That sheriff coming for Thanksgiving?" she asked Marigold.

Marigold nodded as she peeled potatoes.

Sugar sat down in the chair in front of Marigold and leaned toward her. "Marigold, I have to hand it to you. You are playing your cards just right. A sheriff is very respectable. People see him hanging around and they may forget your past and accept you back into society."

Marigold stopped peeling the potato and looked into Sugar's shrewd face. Sugar was disgusted to see the same vacuous expression it always seemed to wear.

"Marigold, someday you will have to leave this house. Someday your baby is going to have to go to school. You cannot hide forever. You have to start thinking of the future. You must be careful who your friends are. The sheriff is a good start. Maybe some time we could even have the mayor over."

"I don't know what you're worried about," Marigold said in a soothing voice. "I'm sure Holcombe will find the marriage license and set everyone straight. He sent a lawyer over here the other day saying they've got someone on it at the county courthouse and they're going through all the records. It's just filed wrong, that's all. Once that turns up, I'll be back in my own house again. He promised."

Sugar snorted. "Marigold, when God gave out brains you must have been in the outhouse!"

Marigold began to peel again and looked down at the potato but Sugar saw a tear glistening in her eyelash.

Joe Brownfield came later that day. There was so little remarkable about him that Sugar didn't believe she could describe him to someone if they asked her. He wasn't dark and tall like Homer. His eyes didn't sparkle the way Homer's did, his smile wasn't crooked and endearing. He was just typical.

Before every meal, Beulah always insisted that every head at her table bow for grace; sometimes there were as many as seven or eight seated there. Today, there were just the three women and Joe, and being as it was a holiday, Beulah made sure the prayer was extra long and special.

As Sugar's stomach growled, her mind wandered and she began to wonder if Homer would be eating anything for Thanksgiving.

After dinner, as they sat at the table, Joe asked her, "You seen Homer lately?"

"Yes."

"What business you got with Satan hisself, bless God?" Beulah wondered.

"We just talk some evenings." Sugar replied a little nervously. Sometimes when Beulah fixed a keen eye on her she wondered if she were clairvoyant. She had seen mind readers at state fairs but she always believed they were fake. Beulah really seemed to have a gift and Sugar didn't like to be on the receiving end of it too often.

"Homer seems to enjoy her company," Marigold interjected quickly. Sugar knew it was for her benefit, and far from being grateful, it annoyed her.

Beulah leaned forward in her chair and put her elbows on the table. "Satan hisself, bless God, is just like a boy I seen in Missouri once. Had the devil in him so deep, he took to jumping around on all fours and barking like a dog. The first time I seen that I knew just what to do. He come a snarling and a barking round me and I took my fist and thumped him hard right on the head. He fell down but when he woke up he never barked again, Hallelujah."

"That may be," the sheriff replied, "but Homer's been thumped with a fist enough."

Beulah folded her tiny gnarled hands and agreed saying, "That he has, Sheriff. That daddy of his is too far gone. They's people that can still be saved and they's people who don't want to be saved and Mr. Guppy don't want nothing but a bottle."

"He won't live long, the shape he's in," Joe commented. "He drinks for days now and when he's done rages against the world and whatever's in his way. After he rages, he passes out for a day and then he starts drinking again. When Homer was littler, he'd hurt him bad. Now that he's bigger, I guess he can take more. Either that or his daddy is getting so he ain't got the strength to tear into him like he used to."

"Why has he not been arrested?" asked Sugar.

"Can't arrest a man with no witnesses and Homer won't talk."

Marigold was looking at her plate, and she sighed convulsively.

"What is wrong with you?" Sugar asked uncomfortable with the conversation.

"I can't stand to hear about any creature being harmed."

Joe smiled at her. "Don't you worry none, Marigold. Homer's got Sugar, here, to keep him company. I've always tried to help him, but my uniform seems to get in the way. He don't trust me like he does you. Young lady, I reckon you're the first friend Homer's ever had."

Sugar felt an intense pang of something, and if her conscience had ever worked before, she would have recognized what it was. What was it about the word "friend" that made her so uncomfortable? She couldn't figure it out, she only knew she was unable to sit still and had to squirm a lot in her chair. It was impossible to meet the honest, dark eyes of the sheriff as he looked at her kindly.

That night, Homer had a fresh set of bruises. Now that his summer tan had faded, they seemed more prominent, more pathetic in the moonlight. "Homer, your daddy thrashed you good this time," Sugar stated, shaking her head and handing him a piece of bread left over from dinner.

It was gone in three bites and Homer shrugged as the shovel bit into the dirt. "Once in a while he gets it into his mind my mama left 'cause of me. When that happens he pounds for all he's worth."

"Why did she leave?"

Homer looked up and stated simply, "'Cause she got the chance."

His shovel clanged against something and they both drew in their breath and stared at each other as if the world had stopped spinning for a second. "Did you hear that?" he asked in a whisper.

Sugar nodded.

He quickly started to shovel again and lifted the clanging object up out of the dirt. It was a mason jar and their hearts stopped. They sat there on the ground their eyes bright with anticipation and Homer began to quickly brush the dirt off of it. Inside, was one quarter. Their eyes met over the jar and despair crept into them.

Homer unscrewed the lid and turned the jar over, the quarter dropping into his filthy palm. He looked at it then handed it to Sugar. "You take it."

"Why?"

"Get yourself something pretty. I ain't got no use for a quarter."

Sugar put the money in her pocket and they both sat there, back to back, feeling sore, in the dust.

Chapter Eleven

Joe Brownfield remained the sheriff of Barmy throughout my childhood. He was very quiet, but the most decent person I have ever had the privilege of knowing, the one person everyone went to when things went wrong.

He was as different from Ensign Lawford as any man could be, but respected in the same degree. He was not wealthy or powerful, but simply honest in all he did and wholly devoted to his wife and children. I admired Joe a great deal as a child but by the time I had reached puberty, I understood the devotion that Marigold had felt toward her first husband in spite of their age difference. The first great love of my life was Ensign Lawford, Junior. He had Marigold's wide blue eyes, but there was something more, an intensity that drew people to him and brought about a deep sense of loyalty. I had heard people speak of his father being the same way. That was why Joe and Marigold almost never married.

Marigold was ashamed of the way she felt when Joe was in the room. Her heart would flutter, she would feel her face flush, and generally, she couldn't think of much to say. As Ensign Lawford's child grew in her womb, her heart was growing warm for another and it made her feel unfaithful and cheap.

Joe's face was always ruddy, even in the winter when the sun didn't burn down. When she asked him about it, he explained, "My family has Choctaw Indian in it. I come from Ralph, Oklahoma." Today, that might not sound like a lot, but in those days it was almost an admission of guilt. To have Indian blood was a disgrace; it coursed through your veins heavily, weighing you down with a deep sense of shame.

Marigold was aware of this when she grabbed his hand and cried, "My granny was Choctaw. She come from Ralph!" Their eyes met in a long, seemingly familiar, glance and she quickly withdrew her hand.

Unable to sleep that night, she crept into the kitchen, made a cup of tea, and watched Homer and Sugar digging under the starlight in the frigid December air. Really, she noted, it was Homer doing the digging while Sugar watched.

"She out there with Satan hisself, bless God?" Beulah asked as she shuffled from her room to check on the bread that seemed to be constantly baking.

"Yes'm."

Beulah cackled a little. "What you reckon they think they'll find?"

"Money."

"Money? What they need money for?"

"Why to leave Barmy, of course."

Beulah sat down in the chair opposite Marigold. "Ain't really the town they're trying to run away from."

Marigold had her hands folded in her lap, but she put them on her knees and leaned forward. "Miz Clinton, I think I should leave Barmy."

Beulah fixed a knowing eye on Marigold. "Why?"

"Why, no reason. Just thinking it might be nice to have a new start, away from . . . everyone."

It seems Beulah had the uncanny knack to hear past the words coming from the mouth and listen to the meaning coming from the heart. Beulah surprised Marigold when she replied, "It ain't a sin to love, child, never has been." She leaned back in her chair, and closed one eye, as was her habit, and said, "They's only two problems with the world as far as I can see . . . they ain't enough love and they ain't enough hate."

"I don't understand . . ."

"Hate ain't indifference. When you hate something, you want it dead, gone."

"Nobody hates wrongdoing. Iffen they did, the world would be a better place. There'd be no soup kitchens, no want, no deprivation. People don't hate poverty and what causes it . . . they's indifferent so it lives and breeds and makes another generation ignorant and hungry."

Marigold's eyes stared uncomprehendingly at her and she continued, "They ain't enough love in the world, either. Look at them two, out there. Never had love in their lives, neither of 'em. They's standing within two feet of it and all they can think of is money." She shook her head and then turned her face to Marigold. "The sheriff's a good man and he'd make a good daddy to that young'un you're carrying."

Marigold gasped. "I couldn't possibly . . ."

"Why?"

"I done been married . . . to Mr. Lawford. He ain't been dead a year."

"Mr. Lawford was wrong to marry you. You was young and he took you away from your kin. It was sin...lust to be plain. It ain't no sin to put an old man behind you and find love while you're still young."

Marigold clasped her hands. "But it feels like sin, Miz Clinton."

Beulah rose from the chair and put a weathered hand on Marigold's still-blooming cheek. "Then it's too soon. Someday it won't feel wrong child, and when that day comes you grab onto love and hold it with both hands." She glanced out the window again and shook her head. "Digging for money when they's so much more." She left Marigold and went back to bed.

If it weren't for Beulah, Marigold would have run away from Barmy, or to be specific from Joe. Her heart would not let loose the feeling she had when he was around. This feeling was nothing like what she had with Ensign. She was afraid of the old man, truth be told. He was worldly and had been with women, many women, while Marigold had never been touched by a man. His hands were cold like death, his lips thin and hard. Her wedding night had been a terrifying ordeal but she had survived it and had forged an understanding with him. She had touched the lonely place in his heart and he, in turn, had loved her.

But she had never truly loved him and for that she was sorry. Joe made her laugh. When he spoke she unconsciously touched his arm or elbow. When he was at the house, it was torture for her to have to leave the room. She treasured the time they had together on his visits. She wanted always to be with him.

The baby kicked her as she sat in the rocker, as if demanding she remember his daddy, as if demanding, much like Ensign himself, her love and her attention. Her head ached with all the thoughts that would whirl through her brain no matter how hard she tried to put them aside. She watched in the moonlight as Sugar pulled Homer's hair. He swatted at her hand but she danced away from him. Marigold sighed. They could have all their hearts yearned for but they were ignorant and hungry, impoverished in too many ways for backward Marigold to number.

Chapter Twelve

Daddy and mama lived in a small house on the outskirts of town. It wasn't much but it did have one great benefit in that there were no lights around it. It was perfect for our stargazing and December was always my favorite month. I would wrap myself in a quilt and lie on the grass, shivering in the cold, but too fascinated to move. Daddy would show me Taurus, Gemini, Perseus, and Orion. We would stay out there, looking up until mama would finally come out, wrapped in a shawl. I remember her face looking down at us, a hint of amusement in her eyes. "Alright you two, tomorrow is a school day."

I would drag myself unhappily to the house and inevitably I paused in the doorway. They would be standing out there in the darkness, his arm around her shoulders and they would be looking up. I know it always reminded her of the first time he had shown her the night sky.

December was coming to a close and nothing of worth had sprung from the dust. Now, the ground was cold and frozen and daddy couldn't get the shovel to dig in, no matter how hard he tried. He sweated and strained in the cold December air and would drop down exhausted beside mama on the back porch. Finally, the ugly truth that there'd be no more digging began to squeeze at their guts.

"Maybe at the January thaw," he had offered the night before as he swung the shovel over his shoulder and started for home.

That wasn't good enough. Sugar paced throughout the house her mind working, trying to seize upon anything. For weeks, she had been taking all of her frustration out on Homer by teasing him ruthlessly. She pulled his hair, she pinched him, she puckered her lips and when he tried to kiss her she'd slap him. Sugar had never been powerless a day in her life. The overwhelming sensation that there was nothing to be done crushed at her and made her mean and spiteful. She snapped at Marigold and was disrespectful to Beulah.

It was Christmas Eve, but instead of brightly colored shop windows, she was offered a dull church service in the next town. When she objected, she was instantly cut off by Beulah who insisted they go to church saying, "Even the devil goes to church on Christmas."

Sugar opened her mouth to respond to this ridiculous notion, but something in Beulah's face made her think better. There was no point, anyway. Nothing was right. Even the weather was odd and foreign. Instead of Chicago's white fluffy snow, she got black dust that rained down making everything sticky with mud. She sighed unhappily.

She was at the breaking point; she had to get out of Barmy before April. It was like being exiled to another planet. Her trunk was in the middle of her room, open, mocking her because there was nothing in it she could sell. There were her daddy's swords but who in Barmy would want them? She would have sold his bones if it would have gotten her a train ticket; anything she owned was up for grabs because she was desperate and angry.

Marigold walked past the door and glanced inside, noticing the opened trunk. She was always a little afraid of Sugar, especially when she was in one of her black moods. "What's in your mind to do?" she asked.

"Whatever I need to," Sugar replied evasively turning back to the trunk with a pout.

Marigold retreated to her room and closed the door and Sugar slammed the trunk closed. Stepping into the kitchen, her eyes scanned the room. In reality, it was a pleasant place with a pot of coffee always boiling and the smell of freshly baked bread always in the air. On this particular day, however, everything about it was hateful to Sugar.

Her eyes landed on Beulah's Bible and a sudden idea formed in her mind. Could the money be neatly tucked inside of there? She went to the back window and glanced at the little stable in the back of the yard. Eve and Mary were missing, Beulah evidently gone on her visits.

Sugar did not hesitate. She crossed the room and sat in Beulah's chair, quickly taking up the Bible. She began thumbing through it page after page. She found a thick piece of paper and pulled it out, hoping against hope some bills were stuffed inside. It was a card, childishly scrawled, on craft paper, a tiny picture of a square representing a church with a woman standing behind the pulpit drawn in green Crayola.

"That was given me by little Verbena Mutton," a voice said. Sugar started at the sound of the voice and her heart jumped into her throat. Beulah crossed the room and looked at the card in her hand.

"Mrs. Clinton! You startled me."

Beulah smiled kindly making Sugar wriggle. "I see you're taking an interest in the Good Book. You read it any time."

"Thank you," Sugar responded weakly. Looking at the card again she asked, "Who is Verbena Mutton?"

Beulah sat heavily in one of the kitchen chairs. "She was a little slip of a girl that I knew in Piney Bluff. She give me that card when I was in jail."

"I do not recall you mentioning that you were in jail."

"No need. It was just a sad misunderstanding. It was at the height of the Piney Bluff Church Wars."

"Church wars? You mean like a holy war?"

"Weren't nothing holy about it."

"But it was a war?"

"Iffen by 'war' you mean were they fighting and shooting at one another, then, yeah, it was a war. The folks of Piney Bluff was a lot like the folks here in Barmy, some good and some not so good. It weren't much that set the whole thing off, a little matter of women speaking from the pulpit. Some said the Good Book was strictly agin it and some saying not.

"I got up one Sunday morning and commenced to sermonizing like I do." Her eyes twinkled a little when she continued, "This here man, Brother Roy, he gets up and starts to preaching too. I shouted him down good, but the next Sunday Brother Roy brought along a nice singing choir and I got shouted down. Before you knew it, we had two services going on, right there in the same little church. Two choirs, two collections, and two ministers pounding and a preaching for all they was worth.

"I reckon it were all a little confusing for the folks in the congregation. Ain't nothin' louder than a Holy Ghost preacher when they is speaking about hellfire and brimstone, and there we both was." She cackled a little in remembrance. "The sheriff, he was of the mindset that women ought not to be preachers so it weren't long afore he came and locked me away. Said I was inciting the folks in Piney Bluff to riot. Next night someone tried to break into the church and they was shot at. Next night someone burnt it down."

Sugar stared. "The church?"

"Oh, yes, the church. The people had no place to go and I reckon to this day they ain't got no church in Piney Bluff. Little Verbena sent me that card the night before they burnt down the jail."

"They burned the jailhouse?"

"Oh, yes, the jailhouse. They was mighty worked up by then."

"And then they released you?"

Beulah rose and took the card from Sugar's hand and looked at it with a wistful smile. She placed it back inside the Bible and took the book from Sugar's lap. "They's plenty of treasure on this here earth, girl, but you got to know what you're looking for."

Beulah sat the Bible back onto the table and went to the stove while Sugar stared after her. Late in the day, she glanced out the window and saw Homer standing in the yard. He beckoned to her so she grabbed her coat and went outside. Homer had no coat, only a ragged jacket with sleeves much too short. He blew on his gloveless hands and smiled at her. "How you doing, Sugar?"

She shrugged sourly, not in the mood for small talk.

"Come with me," he said, grabbing her hand and taking her to the shed.

She followed him and he handed her a box. "Merry Christmas."

Sugar raised her eyebrows in surprise. Inside was a gold chain upon which hung a small golden cross, beautiful, elegant, and expensive.

"Where did you get this?"

"It was my mama's. It's the only thing I have left of her, but I wanted you to have a Christmas present and it's pretty. I thought you might like it."

She turned it over in her hand. Her first thought was the weight of the gold and how much it was worth. For a fleeting moment, she wondered if it would pay for a train ticket. Then her eyes glimpsed Homer's hopeful, bruised face and a feeling of compassion welled up within her so strong it felt like a fist being driven into her throat.

A passing thought that she would never leave Barmy because she was not as hard hearted as Madame flitted through her mind. In a quiet, almost hopeless voice she asked, "Will you put it on for me?"

His clumsy hands gently undid the clasp and put the chain around Sugar's neck. She looked up at him and asked, "Well, how does it look?"

His dark eyes shone with admiration. "It looks real nice on you." Her cheeks were rosy from the cold and her eyes bright and sparkling. "I think an angel couldn't be prettier."

Sugar slid her arms around Homer's neck. He drew back afraid she'd slap him again, but she persistently pulled him down to her until his face was in front of hers.

There were no new bruises, but the remnants of one remained on his jaw. She kissed it gently and she kissed first one cheek and then the other. His eyes looked into hers, they seemed to be questioning and she put her lips onto his and felt him respond by enveloping her in his long arms, holding her against him with all his might, pressing the air out of her lungs. She could feel sixteen years of pain and want in his embrace, sixteen years of needing the touch of another human and being denied. She dropped the small jewelry box and held him tightly.

His grip upon her was tight and desperate, as if he were afraid she would evaporate, afraid she would disappear the way the woman who used to wear the cross did. And Sugar felt this fear and cried out because she realized when the time came she would have to leave him, too. She stepped back and looked into his startled face.

"I'm sorry," he told her. "I'm just a big dumb ox. I scared you."

"No," Sugar said hurriedly. "You do not scare me . . . I do."

He looked puzzled.

She took his large, rough hand and led him to the back porch and they sat down. She turned the hand over and looked at his palm, running her fingertip along it, memorizing every line, every callous, picking at the rough places.

"What are you doing?" he asked with a little laugh.

"I am thinking."

"About what?"

"Why did you give me that cross, Homer? It was your mother's."

He just shrugged.

"No, I mean it. Please tell me."

His face wore a concentrating look as if he couldn't say exactly what he meant. Finally, he replied in a stammering voice, "I wanted to give you something because when my heart beats, I feel you inside of it." He looked down at the hand she was holding, appearing to be embarrassed, his palm remaining open, vulnerable.

Her breath caught in her lungs and her chest felt suddenly heavier, with the weight of another soul lodged in it. She bent her head down and kissed his palm and then reclined against him. They sat silently on the back porch, hand in hand, looking at the bright December stars and an odd feeling of belonging over-whelmed Sugar, something she had never felt before. Not in the hours spent with Madame in her office, not on all of the trains she had ridden with her father. Impulsively, she said, "Homer, if we find the money you could come with me." She was startled by the words that seemed to rise out of a loneliness she hadn't realized.

"Well, I don't know . . ." he said slowly, deliberately.

"Have you ever wanted to be anywhere but Barmy?"

He shivered a little in his ragged coat. "No."

They were silent for a moment and he said, "Look. It's Orion's belt."

"What is that?"

"See those stars. The three in a row." He was pointing at the sky but she was looking at him.

Chapter Thirteen

Growing up, I always loved Christmas. Not for the gifts, because we didn't get much. I loved the Christmas Story due to the fact that it had a star. It was the only verse of the Bible I could recite from memory, "and, lo, the star, which they saw in the east, went before them, till it came and stood over where the young child was."

One year, I sat down at a little footstool at daddy's feet and put my chin in my hands. "How did the star do that, daddy?"

My daddy knew a surprising amount of information about astronomy for someone who quit school in the eighth grade. As long as I remembered, he subscribed to *Sky and Telescope Magazine* and the night sky remained his passion throughout his lifetime. I fully expected him to have the answer.

He leaned forward in his chair and looked down at me, his dark eyes smiling and simply said, "It's a thing no one will ever know. After all, Christmas should be a time of miracles."

I knew that was true, but I knew it wasn't always the case. There were plenty of lean and hungry Christmases when miracles slumbered.

Christmas fell slick and dirty in 1934. Sugar rose from her bed and stared in disbelief at the six inches of black, dusty snow that covered the landscape. There had been dust throughout the fall, but for some reason, this Christmas dusting was heartbreaking. She had wished for something magical; after all, there should be magic on Christmas, not mud. Her thoughts drifted to Chicago and the snow that would glisten as it formed over the lake. Sighing, she reached up to take off her nightgown and realized the cross Homer had given her the night before had become entangled with Dewey Cope's medal. After some maneuvering, she was able to separate them, she put Dewey's medal beneath her dress, but she proudly wore the cross Homer gave her.

It was an odd restless feeling she had that morning. The corn-meal mush tasted blander, the room seemed chillier, Marigold seemed stupider. The gray sky added to her feeling of gloom. She plopped down on a chair and put her chin in her hand.

Beulah entered the room and sat down at the table. Her eyes fell upon the cross hanging around Sugar's neck. "A cross is a proper ornament for you to be wearing, girl. It is a symbol of pure love."

Sugar's hand went to it and she answered, "And it is real gold. I know because I bit it."

Beulah cocked her head to the side and looked at Sugar oddly.

Marigold was frowning. "Miz Clinton, are you sure I need go to church today? My dress is all gapped in the front and I look awful."

Marigold had outgrown the only dress Holcombe Lawford had let her take from the house and it embarrassed her. The church was in Ralph, Oklahoma, and she was sure to see some-one she knew.

Beulah rose and got a large shawl from her room. "You pin this around you and no one will see the gaps."

"Yes'm," Marigold said unhappily gathering the shawl and leaving the room. Sugar knew Marigold's real unhappiness lay in the fact that she did not want to go to church. It wasn't that she was a hater of God, but she knew people were talking about her and it made her feel conspicuous.

They soon left the house and climbed into Beulah's wagon. Sugar didn't mind that they looked ridiculous in a mule-drawn wagon because she knew she would one day leave Oklahoma behind and what the people who lived there thought of her didn't matter. Marigold, on the other hand, knew nothing else, and her cheeks were flushed with shame and embarrassment by the time they pulled into the church lot in Ralph.

Ralph, Oklahoma, was very much like Barmy, though it still boasted a church and a schoolhouse. It was staggered by the Depression; the weight of the dust seemed to suffocate it. The people walked slowly, and talked in hushed tones as if they were at a deathbed, which, in reality, they were. The town itself was dying, the people holding vigil and waiting for the hour.

The church was an austere building, with small strands of garland hung against whitewashed walls. The people were somber as they filtered in, their eyes wide and haunted by the prospect of another skimpy Christmas and another hungry year. They had just taken a seat when a friendly, familiar voice asked, "May I sit with you?"

Joe Brownfield stood there, hat in hand, smiling, his face red even in December's dusty grayness.

"Sheriff," Marigold exclaimed in happy surprise. "I didn't expect to see you here."

She scooted over making room for him on the pew and he sat down. "I'm here having Christmas dinner, or what there is of it, with my folks. And you?"

"Mrs. Clinton has a thing about church on Christmas," Sugar whispered to him over Marigold as the preacher walked in.

The man walked to the pulpit and looked over the room, his eyes landing on Marigold. He opened his Bible and said, "Today I read from the book of Proverbs. 'There are six things which the Lord hates; yes, seven which are an abomination to him: haughty eyes, a lying tongue, hands that shed innocent blood; a heart that devises wicked schemes, feet that are swift in running to mischief, a false witness who utters lies, and he who sows discord among brothers.'" He paused and told the congregation, "'Reproofs of instruction are the way of life, to keep you from the immoral woman. . . . Don't lust after her beauty in your heart, neither let her captivate you with her eyelids.'"

He seemed to be looking at Marigold and Sugar felt her shrinking beside her on the pew. She glanced up. Marigold's face was as white as death, she was trembling a little, her eyes wide and bewildered.

It was at this precise moment that Beulah shot up from the pew, tall and terrible. "Who are you speaking of, brother?" she asked in her high, thin voice.

The pastor appeared startled by Beulah's outburst. He said nothing for a moment and then replied, "I am referring to the harlot in our midst."

Marigold's hand grasped Sugar's. It was cold and sweaty and shaking violently. Sugar looked into her face and felt pity, not a familiar emotion with her, and certainly not a very comfortable one. But, it was one not easily shaken and she found herself squeezing Marigold's hand and trying to comfort her. Joe sat unmoving, dumbfounded, as if he couldn't grasp what was happening.

Beulah said in a thunderous voice, "I didn't reckon on finding a den of vipers in the Lord's house, addle-minded simpletons who listen to idle gossip and judge in the place of God." She raised her hand in the air; her index finger pointed straight up and shouted, "Only He can judge the heart. God have mercy on your souls for the wrong you do this lamb today."

She rose to leave, grabbing Sugar's dress and lifting her from the pew forcefully. Marigold rose mechanically and they all stepped around Joe who remained in the pew looking bewildered.

Beulah paused at the doorway. "One thing I learned in my life is this, God is love, and when you love your brother you's in his light and when you don't you's in the dark. God saw fit to set one example for his children . . . an example of love." She placed her hand on the humiliated forehead of Marigold. "This innocent dove don't even know how to sin." She pulled Marigold out of the door and they made their way across the parking lot, Sugar trailing behind.

Marigold was too shocked to even cry. "He said I was a harlot," she said staring ahead with glazed, unseeing eyes.

They were at the wagon when Joe caught them, running. "Marigold," he called.

She paused and turned to him, her eyes rimmed red, but no tears falling from them. He removed his hat and told her, "I'm sorry. I'm sorry that happened. Stupid hicks. They just listen to any old gossip and take it to heart like it was the gospel truth."

Marigold didn't seem to see him. "He said I was a harlot," she repeated.

He helped her into the wagon and they began the long drive home to Barmy. The wagon ride home was silent for the first half. Finally Sugar said, "Well, Mrs. Clinton, I must say church was more interesting than I thought it would be."

As they arrived, Sugar and Marigold noted there was a long white envelope on the front porch. It was addressed to Marigold.

She opened it and then asked Sugar, "Can you read this to me?"

Sugar took the paper and read, "It says, 'Dear Miss Starling.' Who is that?"

Marigold's face was stricken. "That's my maiden name."

"Oh." She continued:

Dear Miss Starling,

We regret to tell you that upon close examination of the court records in Beaver County, Oklahoma, no abstract or copy of any marriage record has been deemed to exist. With this in mind, Holcombe Lawford wishes to notify you that the house that you lay claim to will remain in his possession. In addition, there can be no legal claim upon any of the property or monies that belonged to his father, the late Ensign Lawford. In view of this unfortunate fact, the child you are carrying cannot, at this time or any other, be considered a legal heir and will have no share in the proceeds of the estate.

Sincerely,
Mr. Duncan Bent, Esquire

Marigold reeled backward and Sugar caught her just before she would have fallen off the porch. "Sugar, how can he?"

"He just wants all he can get."

"But it's not the money. . . . how can he be so cruel? Everywhere I go I'll be labeled a slut and whore, everywhere my baby goes he'll be labeled a bastard." Her hands covered her face and she began sinking. "How can I stand it?"

Sugar helped her to bed. Marigold was awakened some hours later by the sound of voices. A heavy step paused uncertainly in the doorway.

"Marigold?" a deep voice said in a whisper.

She sat up and saw Joe standing there. Her hands went up to smooth her hair down and she started to climb out of bed. "Don't do that," he said in protest. "I just come over to see how you were."

"Thank you," she said her face pathetic in the sliver of moonlight that streamed in the window.

He came in and sat at the end of the bed. "I read the letter Lawford's lawyer sent."

"How could I have been so stupid? There was a minister and everything. Holcombe and my mama witnessed it. I would have never stayed if I'd have known we wasn't married."

Joe absentmindedly picked at a thread hanging from the blanket. He shook his head and told her, "The thing is this, Holcombe Lawford is a sneaky little bastard but Ensign never was. I can't believe he'd lie to you about something like that . . . he never lied about anything. He never pretended virtue before; everyone knew what went on in that house, he was proud of it. He might have been wild, but he was never unprincipled."

"Then you believe me?" she asked in a small voice.

He looked into her face. "Of course, I believe you."

Marigold felt like a crushing boulder had just been lifted from her chest. She took his hand and squeezed it. "Thank you."

He rose to leave. "Here," he said picking up something that had been beside him on the bed. It was a box of candy. "I know how you like sweets. Merry Christmas."

Her eyes shone. "That was so kind. I can share it with Beulah and Sugar."

Joe paused in the doorway and looked back at her smiling. "I knew you would."

Chapter Fourteen

People can generally be broken into two groups; those who can keep themselves amused and those who are constantly in need of others for entertainment. My daddy had always found ways to amuse himself, some good, like learning about the constellations, and some not so good, like burning Skinny Nichols' haystack and flipping Griff Pyle's outhouse. Mama, on the other hand, was at the mercy of everyone around her for diversion. She could never keep herself amused and Barmy, with its monotony, made each day feel like everlasting torture.

The monochrome days of January made her sharp and heartless. Her thoughtlessness caused Marigold to cry, Beulah to pray, and daddy to lust. She passed the dull nights with him out under the stars, caught in a steamy embrace that kept her highly entertained and him panting and yearning. She was a tease and a flirt, he could never get enough but he couldn't put her away. He would come round every night, hankering for her, and the same scene would be replayed, his hand would stray or his lips move and he would be rewarded by a stinging smack on the cheek. One was left diverted and one miserably unsatisfied.

Sugar also tortured Marigold. She got no pleasure from it, she knew it was the same as kicking a puppy or drowning a kitten, and yet, she was so frustrated she didn't try to stop. All around her was weakness and stupidity.

Beulah eyed her sharply one afternoon after Sugar had, once again, prompted Marigold to retreat to her room in tears. "Girl, I'm wanting you to run an errand to town for me."

Sugar liked going to town. It was as pointless as everything else, but at least it was someplace different.

"I want you to see Miss Pet Henson at the dry goods store. She been saving flour sacks for me. Marigold needs a new dress."

"And you use flour sacks?" Sugar asked in disbelief.

Beulah nodded and Sugar began to laugh. "The widow of the richest man in town wearing a dress made out of a flour sack." She shook her head. "He must be rolling in his grave."

"Mr. Lawford didn't provide for his widow, God have mercy on him for it. No one expects to go when they do. He didn't have things taken care of proper and now poor Marigold suffers."

At that precise moment, Sugar heard a stifled sob coming from Marigold's room. That stupid uncomfortable feeling she had acquired since arriving in Barmy pricked at her again.

She walked out into the cold January air. It was one of those gray days where the sun seemed to not want to come out into the cold. The light was dusky and bright, at the same time; silver shadows flitted under the thick, cloudy sky.

She met up with Homer at the street and they walked toward town together. Homer had no coat, and as usual, his long arms stuck out of the bottom of his skimpy jacket. His hands were chapped and red from the cold, their breath wet and smoky.

"When is that January thaw that I have heard so much about coming?" she asked him as they walked. Homer walked fast, partly because of the length of his legs and partly because he was cold. It took a little effort for Sugar to keep up with him but she was very practiced at hiding any kind of weakness or discomfort.

"Don't know."

"You sure it is coming?"

He shrugged.

They walked ahead, Homer with his head down and Sugar trotting alongside; they passed the cemetery and came to the train tracks. Here, Sugar paused, looking first one way and then the other. "Why does the train no longer stop in Barmy?"

"What would it stop for?" Homer asked practically.

Sugar stared at him in frustration, her jaw clinched and her eyes sparking. "Homer, please say something other than yeah, no, and I don't know. If I do not find someone to talk to in this town I am going to start walking down these tracks, ticket or not. I will walk to the next town and sell my body to the first damned cowboy willing to pay for it to get a train ticket."

"Shut up Sugar," Homer replied. "You're not going to do that. We'll find the money when the ground softens." He paused and said uncertainly, "That is . . . if you still want to."

Sugar stared at him in disbelief. "What do you mean if I still want to? Of course I want to. I am losing my mind here. This town is eating me alive!"

"You sound stupid."

"Well, then I guess I finally fit in."

She marched ahead and he quickly caught her. "What's wrong with you, Sugar? So what if you're stuck here? You've got a roof over your head and food to eat."

"And you think that is enough?" she shot back angrily.

He stammered a little when he answered, "I guess I hoped it was." His head bent back down and he pulled his cap down over his eyes and continued on in silence.

Sugar scratched the back of her neck in frustration. What was wrong with her? She made Marigold cry and now she had hurt Homer's feelings.

"Homer, stop, please wait for me."

He paused in his steps and town came into view. She glanced at his face, there was hurt written there even if he said nothing. There were times when she genuinely hated herself.

"I have to go to Henson's Dry Goods store. You know where that is?"

"Next door to Wiley's," he mumbled.

Miss Pet Henson was a short, fat lady with pink hair. It was all Sugar could do to keep her mouth from gaping open when she saw it. It sat on top of Pet's head like a big pink monument to a scheme gone wrong and reminded Sugar of cotton candy. Pet wore black glasses and had a large mole on her cheek. It became evident why Pet had never married, but her unfortunate appearance became easier to overlook once a person got acquainted with her. She had a kind, generous heart, and always mindful of eternity, saw to it years ago that she was baptized not only in the name of the Father, Son, and Holy Ghost, but also in the name of Jesus, just to make sure she had all the possibilities covered.

Sugar approached the counter and was shocked when an amazingly beautiful voice came from the pink-haired woman. "Well, hello, dearie. You must be Sugar."

"Yes, ma'am," Sugar said, trying to hide her amazement.

"Miz Clinton told me you'd be in for the flour sacks. I've been saving them for her after the flour goes into the bin." She shook her head. "Poor Marigold, to have to resort to this. Even her mama, as poor as they was, never had to make her children's clothes from flour sacks. She always had money set aside for material, but maybe that was her undoing in the long run. First time Mr. Lawford saw Marigold she was wearing a new dress. Maybe he thought she was higher up in society than she really was. Such a good girl, and so beautiful, to have to come to this."

She left the room and went to the back to collect the flour sacks and Sugar perused the contents of the quaint store. Homer was sniffing a cigar and Sugar made him put it back. "Homer, how much material do you think it would take to make Marigold a dress?" she asked curiously.

"She's awful big," Homer offered.

Sugar went to the wall where bolts of fabric were hanging. Homer walked up behind her and finding one in a dark shade of pink said, "This is like your costume. I like this color."

Sugar shook her head. "But, not for Marigold." She noted a bolt of fabric, tossed on the floor, it was a pale blue covered with small white daisies.

Miss Henson came back in with the flour sacks. Sugar winced at the rough, ugly red and white checkered material. Pet was looking at them sadly. "At least she'll only have to wear this until the baby's born and she can fit in her other clothes."

Sugar could not take her eyes from the gaudy canvas. "How much for the blue fabric on the floor?" she blurted.

"Why, I ain't priced it yet . . ."

"How much would it take to make a dress for Marigold?"

"Well, I couldn't say . . ."

Sugar took a deep breath and before she could change her mind, reached into her pocket pulling out her own three dollars and seventeen cents, all the money she had. "I will give you three dollars and ten cents for enough fabric to make a dress fit for the widow of Ensign Lawford."

Pet Henson's eyes grew wide. "Where'd you get the money?" She looked at Homer suspiciously. "He didn't steal it did he?"

Homer's face darkened but Sugar quickly assured her, "No ma'am, this is my money . . . or I should say it was my daddy's money."

Everyone in town knew that Pet Henson was a good soul but a terrible business person. Not only did she sell Sugar at least four dollars' worth of dress making material, she gave her bunting and some soft material for baby things.

Sugar left the dry goods store carrying her packages and feeling amazingly good considering she was more trapped in Barmy, Oklahoma, than ever before.

They walked home together, and as they paused at the train tracks, Sugar told Homer, "I got something for you, too."

He was surprised when she handed him a cigar. "You ever smoke one before?" she asked him.

"Once," he answered.

"Me too."

He smiled delightedly. "Did you like it?"

"I did."

"Want to share it with me?"

"Yeah," she answered in a delicious slang that sounded like Barmy.

Chapter Fifteen

It was noted by the inhabitants of Barmy, Oklahoma, that several changes occurred in my daddy throughout the winter of 1934. He stopped raising hell, to the disappointment of those who had predicted prison for the boy and hated to be proven wrong, and he began to look presentable. Suddenly the filthy ragamuffin was always clean, his face shaven, his hair combed, his teeth brushed. People began to take notice of this, and one person, in particular was Saucy Martin, the town's bootlegger.

Homer's daddy, Linford Guppy, had been drunk for fifteen years. He was drunk throughout prohibition, he was drunk for every birthday, every Christmas, and he was drunk for the whole of World War I.

He paid for his moonshine compliments of a Spanish-American war pension, even though he was too young to fight there. While he would have liked, as a young man, to tell people he was one of Teddy Roosevelt's rough riders, in reality, he fought in the Philippines some years later and spent most of his time there in the hospital due to a severe case of typhus. This typhus was deemed the cause of his inability to work, thus every month he collected a pension for a war he never saw.

At one time, he had a bootlegger, a nice respectable man from Tulsa, Oklahoma, by the name of Josiah Brumley, who got his moonshine from a less respectable man by the name of George Kelly. After the arrest of Mr. Kelly, Mr. Brumley decided that bootlegging was too dangerous for him. He turned his operation over to Hal "Boss" Martin and Hal, in turn, was arrested shortly thereafter.

Boss Martin was not bright, but he left his operation in the hands of his more than capable wife, Saucy. Saucy made it a habit of delivering her wares in the company of her children, Autry and Bing. With this kind of cover, not to mention the fact that she had the face of an angel and the heart of a gangster, she was never molested by the FBI and she grew her husband's bootlegging business tenfold in his absence. After the repeal of prohibition, it became easier to track down the moonshine; Saucy would travel into Texas or New Mexico to get it, although the best corn liquor was still made right there in Oklahoma. But Oklahoma remained a dry state and it was no less dangerous to bootleg alcohol after the days of prohibition than during.

Saucy was a young woman, barely twenty-five, with two sons, aged six and four, and she had been bootlegging for four years. She had red hair, cut short and bobbed, and wore lipstick that matched. Her hat and suit were always clean and crisp and her boys dressed in knickers and caps. To see them driving down the road, one would think they were a nice family traveling to church.

But no church would have Saucy, so she created her own sort of redemption by helping the wretched, hopeless refugees that were casualties of the Great Depression. In her own audacious style, she gave what she thought would provide the most comfort: cigarettes, alcohol, toys for children, bawdy humor for the downtrodden, broth for the sick. She was both generous and cunning, where money was short, she required exactly what could be afforded, where money was plentiful, she required more. Linford Guppy got no mercy from Saucy as she had long ago learned to hate him for his treatment of Homer.

Sugar was surprised when she glanced out of the window and saw a Model A parked in front of the Guppy household. Curiously, she walked to the porch and spied Homer standing out front talking to a young woman.

The woman was looking into Homer's face, her palm against his chest, and Sugar thought she was standing closer than was necessary. Sugar crept from the porch and went to the fence row. Here, she overheard Saucy say, ". . . a fine man. Your daddy don't deserve the care you take of him."

"I'll leave him someday. But not right now."

She shrugged her shoulders. "If you change your mind, you know I'll be back in a few weeks. With Boss in the pen, it gets mighty lonesome at my place at night. You think about it." She opened the trunk of her car and reached inside, pulling out a winter coat. Smiling, she held it against Homer and said, "I'll be durned if this thing is too small. You grow every time I see you."

She handed him the coat. "Still it's a sight warmer than what you've got on now. Take it."

Homer looked unsure. "You sure?"

"Yeah, Homer. Take it."

"Thank you."

She touched his arm and gazed into his face. "Don't forget my offer."

"I'll think on it," he promised.

Sugar watched as Saucy climbed into the car. Two little boys could be seen hanging out the window as the car drove off calling, "Bye, Homer."

A curious sensation came over Sugar as Homer and the woman talked, an inexplicable anger and fear. She quickly walked over. "Hello, Homer. I like your coat."

He had just put it on and was looking at the sleeves. "They's almost long enough," he said in satisfaction.

"It seems warmer, too."

He nodded his head.

"Who was that woman?" Sugar asked trying to sound nonchalant.

"That was my dad's friend"

"Friend?"

"It was Saucy Martin, his bootlegger."

"What did she want?"

"She was bringing dad's booze."

"Was there anything else?"

Homer looked at her curiously. "Why?"

"I just thought I heard something . . ."

He shrugged. "She just asked me to do something for her, that's all."

Sugar's heart began to race and her chest felt cold and hollow. "Are you? Are you going to do something for her?"

"I can't decide. I really don't think so, though."

"Homer, she is too old for you," Sugar blurted artlessly.

Homer looked at her uncomprehendingly. "What?"

Sugar took a breath and said in a rush, "I mean, I know you are a fine-looking man, and I can see why she might want you around, with her husband put away, but Homer, she is a married woman with kids and everything."

He stared at her for a moment and Sugar was dismayed to see a glint of mischief in his smiling dark eyes. He pulled his coat sleeves down until they were almost long enough and smoothed the front of it. "I am a fine-looking man, ain't I?"

Sugar felt herself blush. "Homer, stop it."

He laughed a little. "What'd you think she wanted?"

"Why, I thought she wanted . . . well, I guess I thought she wanted you."

"Maybe she does. Just 'cause you don't, don't mean no one else does."

Sugar was dismayed. "Homer, tell me what she wanted. Stop making fun of me."

"She wanted me to come stay with her and the boys until Boss gets out of the pen. They's been prowlers around her cabin and wild beasts and she wants the boys to go to school and is afraid to leave them at home alone when she makes her runs into Texas. She just wanted me to stay on and help out and she thinks I'd be better off away from my dad."

Sugar noted that there were fresh bruises on Homer's face. Her heart sank as she realized that Saucy Martin was right.

"And what do you think?" she asked in a voice of dread.

"Oh, I know I'd be better off away from my dad. But, it's been nicer around here lately."

Sugar's blue eyes sparkled at him. "Really?"

"Yeah. Still, Saucy's a beautiful gal . . ."

"Homer!" Sugar protested.

"Well, she can't dangle from a tree by her teeth now can she? That's a particular habit you have that I enjoy."

"Oh, shut up," Sugar said putting her arms around his waist and laying her head on his chest.

Chapter Sixteen

L iving through the Dust Bowl did odd things to people. My mama always had the notion that Vaseline was the cure for every ill. Growing up, we used it for cuts, burns, chapped hands and lips, diaper rash, and constipation. I never understood her affinity for petroleum jelly; as a teenager I thought it was just because she was ignorant. As I learned more about the times she lived through, however, I began to understand her.

It seems in 1935, the dust grew even thicker. Days would go by without seeing a clear sky and it began to gnaw at the fortitude of every man, woman, and child living in the panhandle. Even those with strong constitutions, who seldom complained, were being cannibalized by it, eaten raw by the darkness and the suffocating dust that made even breathing an almost impossible chore.

"I believe February is the cruelest month there is." Marigold declared, looking at the grayness of yet another dusty day.

Beulah looked up from putting the finishing touches on Marigold's blue dress. "Why is that, child?"

Marigold turned from the window and her eyes held a subdued excitement, a glimpse of what she might have been had poverty not taught her subjugation so long ago. "Can't you smell it? Every once in a while I smell spring, but then it goes away and I can't find the smell again." She sighed sadly. "Today smells like snow."

"In Chicago, spring just smells like mud," Sugar remarked dryly.

Marigold closed her eyes and breathed deeply. "Here, spring smells like dust and rain and wildflowers. It smells like animals and afterbirth and mildewed hay."

"And those are good smells?"

"Yes."

Sugar was doubtful. "Last spring, I got to go to the Shedd Aquarium. You know what that is?"

Marigold shook her head.

"It is a fine big building and inside of it are fish from all around the world. It is a beautiful sight."

Beulah bit the thread with her teeth. "The fishes got a house and they's people living on the streets in Chicago."

Sugar started to speak and then stopped, sitting on her chair with an unusual thoughtful frown.

"Come here, Mrs. Lawford," Beulah instructed Marigold. She held the dress in front of her and stated, "I think that's gonna fit real nice." Turning to Sugar, she added, "When you give, God blesses you tenfold. Don't be forgetting that, girl. The Lord seen that good deed you did and you'll be rewarded."

"My reward will be seeing Marigold beautiful again in her new dress," Sugar responded with uncharacteristic graciousness.

"Shall I try it on?" Marigold asked.

"It's ready," Beulah told her and Marigold scampered to her room.

Looking at Sugar, Beulah declared, "The Lord loves a cheerful giver."

"Do you know, that was the first time I ever purchased anything for somebody else? I never bought my daddy anything and I never bought Madame anything. It seems silly to me, but it did feel good."

Marigold came skipping into the room wearing her dress and spun around childishly. "What do you think?"

"It fits right nice," Beulah told her.

Marigold turned to Sugar who had tears in her eyes. "What's wrong, Sugar?" she asked in alarm.

Sugar's hand quickly went across her cheek. "Nothing, Marigold. You look lovely."

At that moment, a knock sounded at the door. Sugar glanced out the window and said, "The sheriff is here."

Marigold's face flushed red. "Should I change?"

Beulah crossed the room to her and put her hand on Marigold's shoulder. "Sit down, child. No need to change. You look nice."

Joe was let into the house and he quickly removed his hat. He had developed a racking cough over the winter and it wasn't going away. He stood there, unable to catch his breath for a moment as the raspy cough sounded from his lungs. His face grew redder and then pale and finally he stopped and was able to catch his breath.

Then, his old smile covered his face and he said, "Morning, ladies."

Sugar brought him a chair and he sat down thankfully. "Sorry about that," he apologized for the coughing. "This dust goes right through everything." He pulled out a small white mask. "Red Cross give me this, but it don't help. Dust goes inside and just sits there."

Marigold quickly rose, "Can I get you something to drink?" she asked concern clearly written on her face.

He brushed her aside. "No, thankie. Just wanted to see how you all were making out and I wanted to give you this." He reached into a sack and pulled out three small jars of Vaseline. "I wanted to give you each one of these. You rub some of this inside your nose and it helps to keep the dust out. Red Cross is giving 'em out free, but they're goin' fast."

Sugar looked at it doubtfully. "You rub it in your nose?"

"Just smear it around inside," Joe told her.

"With your finger?"

Beulah took the jar and twisted off the cap. She reached her finger inside and smeared the jelly in her nostrils. "Ain't no time to be prissy, girl." When she was through, she rose and told them, "I need to go and make my visits. Thank you for the Vaseline, Sheriff."

Joe rose politely as she left the room and soon Sugar felt a little out of place sitting there with just him and Marigold. Spying Homer on the street, she quickly said, "I best be going, too. I am going to give some of this to Homer."

Again, Joe rose and told Sugar, "It's good for chapped lips and hands, too."

"Thank you, Sheriff." She went outside to share her Vaseline with Homer and it became commonplace to see her sitting beside him on the porch, rubbing it into his red and bleeding hands.

As soon as the house was empty, the old familiar shyness came over Marigold. She rose quickly and offered, "Can I get you some coffee?"

"No. I'm fine, thank you."

She sank back into the chair and they were silent. Then, at the same time, Marigold said, "Fine weather, we're . . ." while Joe said, "It's a nice day . . ."

Again, they were silent. Trying again, Joe said, "Smells like spring isn't far away."

Marigold smiled at her hands. "I think it smells a bit like snow today."

"I was thinking the same thing on my way over."

The momentary silence was broken by Joe saying, "You look nice today. Is that a new dress?"

Marigold blushed. "Yes. Beulah made it for me. Sugar bought the material."

"That was right nice of her."

"Yes."

Joe glanced at the room and noticed someone was knitting baby booties. "You getting ready for the young'un?"

Marigold nodded. "I've made a few pairs of booties and a cap. I need to start on some sleeping clothes."

She had been looking over at the booties, but when she turned back she saw Joe staring at her intently. His feet were shuffling, he seemed uncomfortable. Finally, he said, "Marigold, you know I care for you an awful lot. Iffen when this baby is born, you want any help, or you need a man around, I'd be glad to do anything."

Marigold's face softened into a grateful smile. "Why thank you, Sheriff. That's nice to know."

He crossed the room and sat beside her. "I don't mean as sheriff." He seemed to be thinking of the words to say. "I know Mr. Lawford ain't been dead long and it's soon to be planning, but Marigold, if you ever want to marry again, I'm here. I'd like for you to marry me." He blew air out of his cheeks and closed his eyes as if he had had relieved himself of a burden.

Marigold's face grew astonished and then stricken. "Sheriff, I don't know. I was raised to believe people should only marry once." Her face flushed miserably and she whispered, "I've been with a man."

Joe's eyes were smiling when he replied, "I think I knew that."

"Don't tease me, Sheriff. I know I'm backward and ignorant. Why would you want someone like me anyway?"

Joe took her hands into his. "Cause you're a good soul and I feel like I've known you all my life. You're what I always dreamed I would find one day; you seem to be my other self."

She wanted to withdraw her hands from his, but was unable to find the strength. They were warm and rough and strong. They felt alive and capable, like they could conquer anything. She remembered the cold, dead hands of Ensign Lawford and felt her heart being torn in two.

She looked into Joe's honest face. Everything about him felt like home. He was her people, he was not Ensign Lawford who came from another land and lived a different kind of life. He was her history, her future.

"Sheriff, I just don't know. It's hard to think right now, on account of the baby." She finally took her hands from his and clasped them before her lips, almost as if she were praying.

"You don't have to say anything today. Just think about it. Will you?"

Her wide blue eyes looked into his and she nodded.

"In the meantime, instead of Sheriff, could you call me Joe?"

That she could do.

Chapter Seventeen

The cold didn't seem to want to let up. It was cold outdoors and cold indoors but the coldest place in Barmy, Oklahoma, was the heart of Holcombe Lawford. As a child, Holcombe was whiny and demanding, as a man he was much the same. In a place like Barmy where a man earned respect for honesty and hard work, Holcombe earned none. He was pale and scrawny and had thin hands—feminine, white, and without calluses because they never did any work. He had his mother's slender build and short stature, his nose was long and thin, his eyes close together, and his cheeks had hollow places that might have been called dimples on a more attractive man. But being attractive mattered little to Holcombe as marriage was not necessary. Holcombe's solace, his only true love, was money, or to be plain, the power it could buy. He calmly sat in his house day after day and watched Barmy shrivel and begin to die, but truth be told, Holcombe liked Barmy best on its knees; from that prospect he seemed even taller.

Everyone in town seemed to hate him; however, Marigold, the person, it seems, with the best reason to hate him, missed him and wished him well. But that was one of the things about Marigold that bothered Sugar; she always thought the best of everyone regardless of how little they deserved it and it was hard for her to dislike anyone. She always found good things in Holcombe Lawford, even though the truth of the matter was there was no good in him.

One morning, Sugar awoke to clear skies. She quickly rose from bed and dressed, going through the usual morning ritual of untangling her cross and medal. Every night, they would become intertwined; sometimes the links of the chains would even meld together. It took her several moments each dawn to unlink them, but she could not bear to sleep without either.

She was walking out the door, fastening the cross when she ran right into the barrel chest of Dewey Cope who had arrived at the door.

"Well," he said his eyes twinkling. "If it ain't my little friend from Chicago."

Sugar smiled up at Dewey. She always liked him. He was strikingly gentle for someone so large and he helped her understand Marigold's loyalty to the memory of Ensign Lawford. There was something so genuine in his speech and movements that she felt instantly at ease whenever he was around.

He looked down and saw the golden cross. "I see you've got a new necklace."

Sugar quickly fumbled beneath her dress bringing the miraculous medal into view. "I still have your medal. I am waiting for my miracle, but so far all it seems to have produced is dust."

Dewey laughed, loud and boisterous. "That medal didn't make the dust, young lady. It was man that made the dust."

"How is that?"

"By taking this here prairie and raping her. We used her like a two-bit whore and when she got sick of it, she up and flew away."

"I am sorry, but I do not understand."

"We farmed her hard year after year. She got tired of it. If you take advantage of something, sooner or later, it ain't gonna stick around to be used no more."

She backed away from him a little and looked up into his face, brows knitted together, lips pursed in thought. "And the earth is leaving?"

"I watch it every day."

The thought that Homer wasn't around as much as he once was briefly flitted through her mind. But how could he be? The dust made it impossible. Still, she had a nagging feeling in her chest that didn't seem to want to go away.

Dewey glanced at the cross hanging from the chain. "That's a pretty cross."

"Thank you."

He looked puzzled. "Ain't no corpus on it."

"I beg your pardon?"

"Corpus. Ain't no body of Christ hanging there."

Sugar's hand went to the cross and she looked down at it remembering Homer's face the night he had given it to her. "Beulah says a cross is a symbol of pure love."

"Love without sacrifice is just a cheap imitation."

Sugar studied his face keenly. "Sacrifice?"

"Sacrifice, offering, whatever you want to call it." He paused then asked, "Is Mrs. Lawford at home?"

"She is in the house."

He removed his hat, eyes still twinkling at her. "I bid you good day, then Miss Sugar."

He went inside and Sugar stood on the porch deep in thought. She plopped down and put her chin on her hand. Was Homer growing tired of being used by her? Was she even using him anymore? He had become the most important thing in her life and she wasn't even sure when or how it happened.

At that moment, a familiar step sounded at the gate and she looked up to see him standing there, smiling his familiar crooked smile. Her heart melted and she hurried to him, looking up into his face with an expression that probably took him by surprise.

Indoors, there was little to smile about. Marigold showed Dewey Cope the letter from Holcombe Lawford's lawyer. As the gentleman read it, he became so angry Marigold was afraid he would kill Holcombe. His face grew red and he threw the envelope on the table with a loud slap.

"The sneaky little bastard," he said in a tone of subdued anger. "He never even told me he did this. Right behind my back he worked it." He swiped his hand across the bottom of his nose. "Damn, him. To send such a letter. I watch him you know," he told her. "I watch him day and night. How he managed this . . ." he stalked angrily across the room and looked out the window.

"I'm sure it's just a mistake," Marigold said in her mild voice.

Dewey turned to look at her. "It's a mistake alright and Holcombe's the one making it. I knew he'd make trouble and I knew what he'd do, but I didn't count on him worrying you with this crap." He sat down in a kitchen chair and scooted it so he was right before Marigold. "Before Ensign died he asked me to take care of you if something ever happened to him. I will, by God. I didn't want you two to marry. I knew no good would come from it for either of you, but he wouldn't listen. I spent a lifetime cleaning up his messes and I don't intend to stop just 'cause he's gone." He rose angrily and ran his hand through his white hair. "Holcombe sent this to you and you with that little one. I'd like to knock that heartless son of a bitch as far as I can send him!"

Marigold picked at her lower lip and then bit it. "Mr. Cope," she said quietly. "I really don't want Holcombe's money. I know I can manage. It's not that . . . but people are talking. I just ain't sure no more. Is it a mistake? Is it possible that me and Ensign was never married?"

Dewey turned to her and shook his head. "You was married, Mrs. Lawford. Don't worry none about it. I'll take care of you, I promise. Ensign was like a brother to me and I loved him. I didn't always agree with the decisions he made, but I always stood by him. Don't let Holcombe worry you no more. Any more letters come from him, I want you to put right in the trash barrel in the yard. You hear?"

Marigold nodded. "Mr. Cope, you know I would trust you with my life."

He crossed the room and patted her shoulder. "I'll see to it that trust is not misplaced." He turned to leave. "Good day to you, Mrs. Lawford."

Chapter Eighteen

February of 1935 was the coldest February on record. Marigold's longed for spring, seemed like it was in no mood to arrive. Desperation began to arrive all along the panhandle, like some vagrant relation not anxious to leave. It came in the form of measles, mumps, and something new called dust pneumonia. In Barmy, they were lucky. Only two people had died. In other places, like Ralph, that number was in the dozens.

Stealthily, sickness stole its way into town, like a ghostly spirit, winding its way into homes and businesses, peering around corners, weaving into families, leaving behind misery. Fear was borne on the wind along with the dust, the houses shut up tight against a killer without conscience.

My mama almost died during the Depression but she never told me. Like other children brought up in the forties, I had to fit together vague pieces of a hidden puzzle to understand things. She never told me she almost died; she didn't need to. I saw it on my daddy's face every time she coughed or got sick, a fear, a resolute memory that would stir in his mind and cause him to fret over her. It seems he brought the sickness to her, an innocent case of measles that became an iniquitous death sentence.

The dust blew more every day. Everyone in the house on Grit Avenue had raw throats and nagging coughs. They couldn't keep the dust out of the house, or out of their bodies.

Homer still wasn't around as much as he used to be. He'd stop by for short visits then he would walk off somewhere and Sugar wouldn't see him again until the next day. After about two weeks of this mysterious behavior, she was alarmed when he showed up flushed and feverish, his eyes red, his face covered in a rash.

"What is wrong with you, Homer?"

He covered his eyes with his hand. "Nothing. Just this light hurts my eyes."

Sugar put her hand on his forehead. It was burning hot. "Homer, you are sick."

He brushed her hand from his forehead. "Ain't sick. It's just a cold."

She was not convinced. "You do not get a rash with a cold. I think you need to get to bed."

At that moment, Joe drove up in his car. He was out in the dust more than most and was growing thin and wasted, his cough rarely letting up long enough to have a conversation. He'd seen plenty of sickness and the minute his eyes fell on Homer's face he shook his head.

"Boy, you got the red measles."

Homer didn't believe him.

"I seen them all over town and I know what they look like." He began to cough. After a moment, he added, "You don't need to be hanging around here getting all these women sick."

Marigold had appeared in the doorway. "It's okay, Joe. I've had them. Have you, Sugar?"

Sugar shrugged. "Nobody told me one way or the other."

Joe looked pointedly at Homer. "You get those from Saucy's boys?"

Homer's face flushed brightly and his eyes moved to his shoes. "Probably. They both had 'em last week."

Sugar's heart fell. She had suspected Homer was living at Saucy's but had been afraid to ask. Her head began to ache. "Is that where you have been staying?" she asked in a weak voice.

He wouldn't look at her face. Staring at his hands, he answered, "She ask me to come help her take care of 'em when they got sick. She still had her runs to do and they couldn't be left alone."

The dull ache in Sugar's head was becoming a painful pounding. "You did not tell me."

He said nothing.

Her eyes closed and her fingertips rubbed her forehead between her eyebrows. She felt cold and hot all at once.

Opening her eyes, she saw Homer looking at her. "You okay?"

She suddenly didn't care where Homer was sleeping or where she was. She didn't care about Chicago or Madame. The only thing she wanted was to lie down and make the headache and the sore throat go away.

"I need to go inside," she murmured, unable to find enough gumption to speak up.

She rose and the porch began to sway beneath her. The next thing she knew, she was leaning against Marigold's body. It was soft and comforting.

Sugar's fever soon climbed dangerously high. People were in and out, but she was oblivious. They would stand in the doorway, shaking their heads and muttering what a shame it was because of her age.

Joe came several times a day, always wishing there was a doctor they could send for and sitting with stricken eyes, because he knew what death looked like and he could see it in Sugar's face.

On the third day, her fever climbed so high that Marigold exclaimed, "Miz Clinton the pillow is burning hot."

Beulah quietly came into the room carrying her sewing scissors and Marigold resolutely held Sugar up while Beulah cut her long beautiful hair. Tears slid down Marigold's face because Sugar had always been so proud of it. She had once told her that every aerial artist had long hair because it made them appear longer and more graceful in the air.

That was the last day Sugar cried out. It froze Marigold's heart because Sugar would cry out, but never called a name. It was then Marigold realized that she had never had anyone to take care of her. Marigold sat with her during the day, Beulah sat with her during the night and Homer slept on the porch haunting the place like a guilty specter.

After that day, the only sound that came from Sugar was the labored wheezing that could be heard anywhere in the house. Marigold would hear it at night as she tried to sleep, and it would break her heart. It was a horrible sound, the sound of life being torn from a strong body.

After seven days the wheezing became shallow and slow, it seemed as if the next breath was too hard for her to take, as if the fighting was becoming too much. That was the day Joe Brownfield went into town to order Sugar's coffin.

Bertha Lorene Cope came that day. She seldom left her home, but her husband had taken a liking to the young woman and she wanted to pray with her. She entered the room with a bottle of holy water and splashing it upon Sugar's head baptized her in the name of the Father, Son, and Holy Spirit.

The miraculous medal had once again become entangled with the cross. Bertha bent down to separate them and then put the cross to Sugar's lips. Making the sign of the cross, she left the house convinced she would never see Sugar Watson alive again.

Marigold came inside from the pump with a bowl of water to bathe Sugar's head and noticed the door was ajar. She peeked into the room and was surprised to see Homer had slipped in.

He was sitting on the floor next to the bed, his long arm draped across her, his cheek on the mattress and his thumb stroking her face.

She entered the room and said quietly, "Homer?"

He glanced up. "I don't want her to be alone when it happens," he said in a choked voice. "She's afraid of the dark."

Marigold stepped out of the room and he slept there that night, leaning on the bed, his long legs impossibly folded under him.

The next morning, Sugar was soaked with sweat. Beulah rushed in, almost knocking Homer out of the way because his legs were cramped and he couldn't move quickly enough.

"Praise be," she exclaimed. "The Lord has spared her on this night."

Marigold came rushing in and when she turned to speak with Homer, he was gone.

Sugar didn't die that night or the next and whether it was Homer that kept her from death no one will really ever know, although Marigold lived her life convinced of it.

Sugar lay there for two more days, the sweat pouring from her, her breathing becoming deeper and more restful. And when she finally woke from that long bout of sickness, the first face she saw was the worn worried face of Marigold Lawford and she was so grateful tears formed in her eyes.

And maybe she would have cried if she had had the strength, but all she was able to do was smile a weary smile and sob a choked, "Thank you" as she grasped Marigold's hand.

Chapter Nineteen

My littlest brother was born in 1944, two weeks before daddy left for the war. He was a breach baby and gave mama some trouble with his birth. Miss Marigold sent me, daddy, and my brothers for a walk.

We walked aimlessly, I really don't think daddy knew where his feet were taking us, and we suddenly ended up at the creek on the outskirts of town. My brothers went to splash sticks at the side of the water, but I sat beside daddy. He had shadows under his eyes and fidgeted nervously. I wanted to ask him if mama would be alright, but I was afraid to. His eyes were clouded with fear and guilt, like mama's suffering was his fault. I'm sure he was remembering that other time, so long ago, when he brought sickness to her.

March arrived in a haze of dust in 1935. There had been only a small amount of snow over the winter and the drought didn't seem to be in much of a mood to let up. The thunder would roll now and then in a tantalizing rumble, but no rain would fall. The dust was ever present, when everyone awoke in the morning, it was in the corners of their eyes, their mouths were gritty with it, noses black when blown.

Sugar's strength was returning a little day by day. She sat in a chair and watched Marigold with a newfound appreciation.

Why Marigold had sat with her so many hours night after night, Sugar couldn't understand. When she had the chicken pox, Madame had sent her to her room and asked her to not present herself again until her health was better. The closest thing she showed to affection was when she told Sugar to take care and not scratch because it would leave a scar.

But Marigold had bathed her, she had fed her, she treated her like she loved her, and Sugar thought that maybe, perhaps, she did. But why she did, Sugar could not understand.

She watched Marigold closely, every day, and there was something in her patient resignation that was fascinating. Every morning, Marigold stuffed rags in the cracks beneath the windows, but the dust came in below them. Then, she wetted the rags and it was better because the dust got trapped and turned into mud, and in turn, the mud kept more dust out. She spent hour after dusty hour, wiping clean the tables, the window sills, the stove. Everywhere she wiped was dusty again, but she doggedly turned around and wiped some more.

For days, it seemed, her face had worn a thoughtful, wistful expression that rendered it even more beautiful in a melancholy way. She would often rise from her seat and walk to the window gazing out over the dusty landscape. She said little, but sighed often and sometimes she would stare at her left hand where Ensign's gold band rested and close her eyes sadly. She was quite large now, the baby she was carrying due within the month. She explained away her weariness by saying the child kicked her in the night while she tried to sleep. But she was dull, listless. She seemed to have lost interest in anything but keeping the dust out of the house. It was a constant struggle and she was losing.

Sugar also watched Homer from the window as he paced in front of the gate, as if walking the picket in some war. Indeed, for him, it was a war, and his mind was the battlefield. A desperate war raged there, the forces of guilt in combat with the forces of love. He knew he gave her the measles and he knew he got them from being somewhere he shouldn't, but that didn't stop the longing he had to see her face and hear her voice.

At first, Sugar liked to see him walking there. In her mind, it would have served him right if she had died. She was angry that he had deceived her, though, in reality, she had known where he had been all along. After several days of this, she couldn't stand the ache of being without him any longer, though she was still impatient with herself for missing him. She asked Beulah if she would invite him in.

As soon as he entered the room, the bruised cheek and bloodied lip told her that Homer, had indeed, moved back home and she hated herself for being glad.

He was nervous and fidgety; he wouldn't meet her gaze no matter how hard she tried to catch his eye. Finally, she asked, "What do you think of my hair?"

His eyes slowly looked up from the floor and rested on her face. There were dark shadows under them, he looked tired and worried and she instantly forgave him for being at Saucy's. "Well?"

His slow crooked smile formed and he said, a little shyly, "I like it."

Sugar smiled a little and admitted, "I hate it."

He sat down and visited with her for the rest of the afternoon. After that, he came and visited with her most days and Sugar realized after the third day that Beulah now addressed him as "Homer."

"My goodness, I have dirt in my ears," Sugar said one day as they were inside during a dust storm. She was desperately trying to knit baby booties and not having any luck. Marigold had tried to teach her, but Sugar had absolutely no patience. Every stitch was instantly taken out and the lack of progress was irritating to her.

Marigold and Beulah both looked up at her exclamation, but neither had anything to say in response. The room remained silent, the very weight of the dust in the air made speech seemingly impossible. It was dark inside and out; even the lantern sputtered and flickered as if the dust were too much for it to fight against.

A knock on the door startled them and Beulah went to open it. Joe Brownfield was on the other side, filthy in his sheriff's uniform, the dust covering every crease, every wrinkle, sticking to the buttons and filling the pockets.

He came inside and removed his hat, revealing a line of clean white skin just below his hairline. After greeting everyone he said, "Come to the door. I want to show you all something."

They got up and joined him at the doorway and he pointed at Beulah's fence. It was glowing; sparks of electricity were jumping from the chicken wire like spirits flinging themselves toward heaven. It was bright and luminous; it stood out against the dust in a spectral way and Marigold gasped.

"What is it?" she asked in a whisper.

"It's called St. Elmo's Fire. It only happens during the more powerful storms, and this one's a doozy." He turned his eyes to her face, they were tender. "I wanted you to see it."

They stood there in wonder, watching the sparks that were colored blue and red. "It's beautiful," Marigold breathed in awe.

His hand instinctively covered hers and Joe and Marigold stepped onto the porch. They watched the dust fly past; the seeds, the hopes and dreams of the farmers, blew past them with devastating fury, but they only saw the beauty of the sparks on the fence. The ugliness of the dirt could wait for the hours when they were apart. Finally, she began to cough and they went back inside, black and wonderstruck.

Putting his hat back on, he told everyone, "Well, I guess I'd best get going. Dust is so thick I can hardly see, but people are probably stranded and I need to make sure they're okay. Damned car shorted out about two miles down the road. I'm sure mine's not the only one."

Marigold went back to the door with him. Her eyes were wide and frightened when she said, "Please be careful."

He touched her arm. "I'm always careful."

He left and Marigold got a wet rag and began, again, the ritual of wiping the dust.

Chapter Twenty

March of 1935 came in like a dusty, bedraggled lion and it gave every indication of leaving in exactly the same way. Mama was young and strong, her recuperation quick and complete. Ten days in that house had upset her coolly controlled world. She found herself in the unenviable position of desperately wanting that which she did not want. She wanted my daddy, she wanted to be with him, to hold him to love him, but she could not stay with him and it made her miserable.

Saucy Martin had been by again, and once more, Linford Guppy had his booze. Sugar was not sure Linford ever left the house; the only proof she ever saw of his existence was the punishment he inflicted on his only child.

Homer stayed away from him as much as humanly possible. He walked all day, he was out most of the night, he was even out in the dust, but he couldn't always be out, and when he was home, Linford took delight in funneling his rage into senseless violence.

Sugar had been at Beulah's long enough to notice the pattern. The beatings were worse shortly after Saucy left, then they got gradually fewer until the day Saucy came back. Then the cycle began again. Sugar had learned to hate the Model A. She hated it because she knew it meant pain for Homer and she hated it because she knew Saucy wanted Homer.

Homer didn't see what Sugar saw. He didn't see the lingering glances, he didn't notice the caresses, and he didn't understand the hunger in Saucy's eyes when she looked at him. Sugar understood it well. It was a hunger, borne from loneliness, from the longing to be touched.

Sugar felt this hunger, now, when Homer kissed her. She felt a need to press close to him and hold him tightly, she wanted to be able to crawl in his skin and be inside of him. She didn't know that she loved him because she had never loved anyone, but she knew she needed him and the need frightened her because she had never needed anything. The thought of Saucy taking him away from her was a constant terror.

Saucy came every three weeks, and every three weeks she begged him to come back. Sometimes the boys were sick, sometimes there was a panther in the creek bed, sometimes there were gangsters on the prowl, but the reasons were not enough for Homer. Nonetheless, Sugar always watched the car zoom away, bouncing on the dusty road, with the little boys hanging out waving. She always studied the car, to be sure there was only one person in the front seat and she always sighed with relief when there was.

She would inevitably join him as he watched it drive off into the distance. "I see Saucy has come again," she would say.

"Yeah."

"What did she have to say?"

"The same thing as always."

"What did you tell her?"

His answer was always the same, "I told her not today."

It was a clear night, with no dust, so Sugar was able to wait for Homer in the yard. He finally showed up with a black eye and a bloody lip. She never asked him what he did to make his dad thrash him anymore. Nothing needed to be done. He sat down and glanced at her out of the corner of his eye. "Sorry, I'm a little late," he said. He was always ashamed of his bruises.

"Homer, has your dad always beat on you?"

"Yeah."

"Why?"

Homer thought for a minute. "I don't know. I guess 'cause he was bigger."

"But you are bigger than he is now."

"Yeah."

She took his hands into hers and held them, peering into his face questioningly. "Then why not fight back?"

He seemed surprised by the question. "Cause he's my dad."

Sugar reached up and kissed his lip, tasting blood. It was bitter and salty, like thick, sticky tears. She felt an overwhelming desire to tuck him away somewhere safe, somewhere that his father could not find.

And, suddenly, an awful pain stabbed at her heart because she knew he could be safe from his father today, if not for her. She put her hand over her chest as this sensation of guilt flowed through her. Madame had told her guilt was a useless emotion, everyone was responsible for their own actions; there was no need to feel bad if things didn't turn out well for them. To Sugar, Madame had always been infallible, the one great right in a world of wrongs. Since arriving in Barmy, however, there were many times Sugar had been forced to doubt Madame's correctness. To Madame, Homer would have been useless, she would have told Sugar to walk past and not look, the same way she did with the young man who lived in Sugar's tenement in Chicago. Sugar always liked him and Madame prevented her from seeing him saying he was Irish, uneducated, and would one day be in a soup kitchen. Had Madame been with her, Sugar would have never spoken to Homer.

She hadn't realized he was looking at her until he asked, "What are you thinking so hard on?"

She glanced up at the swollen eye. Taking a deep breath, she said, "Homer, I think you should go with Saucy next month."

He was silent for a startled moment and then asked, gravely, "Why?"

"Because, she would feed you and clothe you and treat you right."

After a pause, he asked her, "Is that what you want me to do?"

She couldn't answer, there were so many conflicting messages running around her brain. Finally, she artlessly blurted, "Homer, I just want you to be safe, away from your daddy and his drinking. It hurts me to see you bloody all the time." She felt foolish and out of control.

His arm went around her and he leaned his chin on the top of her head. "Don't worry about me, Sugar. I'm used to it, and besides, I ain't sure I don't deserve it."

Sugar pushed him back and looked into his face in surprise. "What do you mean?"

"I mean, maybe I deserve to be beat. I'm sure my mama left cause of me. Dad says my crying drove her off."

"Did you ever think maybe your daddy's drinking drove her off?"

He shrugged.

She put one hand on each side of his face, and kissed him again and his arms went around her. She crawled onto his lap and they kissed there, under the moonlight, almost crying in the desperation to be together as one, to be one spirit, one heart and one soul. Their pain was more than a physical craving, it was the craving to be known to another human, an instinct as old as time, the need to know and be known.

He held her against him; she could feel the beating of his heart through their clothing. And then, his head went to her shoulder, as if the exhaustion of wanting desperately what he could not have was too much for him. His breath was hot and labored, moist against her skin.

They sat on the porch, in the moonlight, riddled with pain because there could be no way for them. They had no money, no future, only an unrequited ache that made them both miserable. His head went up and he looked out across the dusty field behind Beulah's house. She laid her face on his shoulder and snuggled against his neck, sighing with bittersweet pleasure because tonight he was here with her and tomorrow must not be thought of.

After a moment she asked, "Will you go?"

He turned his eyes to hers. "Not today."

Chapter Twenty-One

Now, most days had dust. It was like an abysmal spirit, dark and unfathomable, that haunted the souls of Barmy. People had to stir outside, but when they did, there was always the need to be looking over one's shoulder, the feeling of expectation that the sky would burst above you and the dust swallow you up. Folks were on edge and nervous. No one could stand still when the sun shone. They would go about their business, wringing their hands, looking to the sky, and hoping the blackness wouldn't eat them alive.

The dust was hard on Marigold, the baby pressed on her lungs from below and the dust tried to fill them from above. She tried to keep the place tidy, but she would often run out of breath after just a few moments and need to sit down. She was tired and troubled. Joe coughed continuously—the mask the Red Cross had issued did not keep the dust out; he inhaled it every day as he was out in the storm.

"God has done a terrible thing," Marigold remarked in despair one Saturday afternoon as she sat down to catch her breath after dusting the kitchen table. A pattern had almost developed. For every clear day there were almost two dusty ones. It made life impossible.

"God don't do terrible things," Beulah corrected. "Man done this to hisself."

Joe came for his daily visit. He was thin and weakened, every hour he was helping those stranded, destitute souls trying to escape the dust and finding themselves swallowed by it. It was a slow death, a sandy drowning.

He sat down, coughing, and then smiled a weary smile at Marigold. His eyes were still bright and sparkling, his skin still young and ruddy, but now he was thin, his body like an old man, stooped and starved for oxygen.

Marigold sat beside him, concern written clearly on her face. "You getting by okay?" he asked her.

"I'm fine."

He was worried because, in reality, Marigold could give birth at any time now. "If that baby comes during a dust storm, what will you do? That dust comes right through the boards of this place. How will the mid-wife get here?"

Marigold forced a smile. "I don't know, but I won't worry about it." The smile faded and her voice was low. "Really, Joe, there ain't nothing I can do."

He leaned forward. "The jail house is stone. The dust don't come into it like it does these boarded up shanties. You could stay there."

Marigold's face grew white. "Live in the jailhouse?"

"It's just an idea," he told her. "You'd be spared some of the dust." He began to cough, his body racked with the force of it. Marigold watched helplessly, her face stricken. Finally, the coughing subsided and Joe spit into his handkerchief. He closed his eyes and caught his breath, then told her, "Will you at least think about it?"

She nodded, her ears still ringing with the sound of the harsh coughing.

A knock at the door made them all jump and Sugar went to open it. Saucy Martin was on the other side. Amazingly enough, she was clean and crisp and looked as respectable as always, as if the dust wasn't calculating enough to land on her.

Saucy made it a habit of avoiding anyone unconnected with her bootlegging, as, in her opinion, she had been judged and humiliated enough. Only those souls who needed her seemed to understand, and for her, that was enough. This visit was unexpected and unprecedented.

Sugar let her in and Saucy's eyes landed on the sheriff. She and Joe had an understanding. Joe knew what it was she did for a living and he understood why she did it. He never saw her deliver anything; he never made it a point to look.

Her smile was brilliant: white teeth, clean white skin. She stood out amongst the drab dirt like a last vestige of pure December snow, unmelted on the mud.

"I'm sorry to barge in," she said in a clear voice, "but Sheriff, I got business with you."

Joe began to rise but she quickly noticed the condition he was in and said, "Don't get up. It can be done right here." She motioned out the door and her boys Bing and Autry came in, between them a little girl of about three years of age.

"Sheriff, this here girl's name is Etta Esmerelda. Her daddy give her to me for a bottle of hooch. He told me his wife done died of pneumonia and he couldn't raise her and he was gonna drink the hooch and blow his brains out."

Joe quickly rose, grabbing his hat. "Maybe I can stop him . . ." he began.

"Oh, the deed's done," Saucy told him matter-of-factly. "I heard the shot myself. Ain't no point in rushing out there now."

Joe sat slowly back down and began, once again, his racking cough. Saucy waited until he was finished to say, "I want to keep this child. Always wanted a girl and Boss gonna be locked up for a long while yet. What do I need to do to make it all legal like? You know I can afford her."

"You need to get to the courthouse and fill out some papers." Joe replied.

The little girl stood in the room, with wide startled eyes, filthy and clothed in an onion sack.

Saucy nodded and said, "Thanks, Sheriff. You'll find her daddy down in the creek bed by his truck." She took the little girl's hand and left the house followed by Bing and Autry. The filthy little girl offered an interesting contrast to Saucy and her boys.

Joe grabbed his hat and looked unhappy. "I reckon I got a body to retrieve," he told everyone. He patted Marigold's shoulder and said, "Think about what I told you. It would offer better shelter for you and the little one."

She forced a little smile, nodded, and watched from the doorway, as he slowly walked to his car, hunched like an old man. Her eyes went to the sky, it was clear for now, but she knew the dust was waiting, stalking them all like a spider, and there was no escaping the web.

Chapter Twenty-Two

As a child, I looked up to and admired Mr. Dewey Lee Cope. He brought to my mind visions of cowboys, presidents, or maybe, General Patton or Eisenhower. He smelled of pipe tobacco, peppermint and corn liquor, his cursing always a source of enjoyment to my brothers who emulated him whenever mama wasn't around.

Dewey was proud that he had never produced anything but sons, proud that they were all just like him and proud that they all went to work before they attained their teenage years. They worked as field hands, they worked on oil rigs, they walked the fences for the ranchers. That being said, Holcombe Lawford, Ensign's only child, never did anything and because of it Dewey couldn't stand the sight of him.

Because of his daddy's hard work, Holcombe Lawford was one of the few Americans in 1935 who had the privilege of paying federal income taxes. He set Dewey to the task of taking care of this as he didn't like to be bothered with details and Dewey made details his business.

Sugar had just plopped down on the porch, with her chin in her hand when she saw Dewey walking to the house at a rapid pace, his eyes bright with excitement.

"Good morning, Miss Sugar," he said removing his hat and running his hand through his thick white hair. "Is Mrs. Lawford at home?"

Marigold seldom left the house but on this particular occasion she had gone to visit an elderly woman with Beulah.

Dewey looked disappointed. "I wanted to see her. Can you tell her the answer to our questions fell in my lap today? Can you tell her that?"

Sugar looked at Dewey in surprise. He was obviously excited. "What do you mean?"

"I mean I think I can take care of her problem. But I have to go into Oklahoma City. Holcombe's got Beaver County bought up good and tight and I'd trust any judge or lawyer here about as far as I could throw 'em. Can you tell her where I went and what I'm doing?"

Sugar nodded.

"One more thing," he said taking his hand and reaching into his jacket pocket. "Jewel Wiley asked me to give you this telegram. Said it came in about an hour ago." Dewey handed her the thin white envelope. Her shaking hands took it; the envelope seemed like dead weight, heavy and wooden.

"Well, I'm off," he said cheerfully. "Hope to be back in a few days." He started to leave and then turned back. "You still got that medal, missie?"

She smiled and her eyes went back to the envelope. "Yes," she replied. "Perhaps today my miracle has happened."

His eyes twinkled. "I hope it has. Good day."

Sugar went to her room to read the telegram. She didn't want Beulah, Marigold, or especially, Homer to catch her and see what it said. She closed the door behind her and sat on the floor with her back against her trunk, staring at the envelope, frightened to open it. What if Madame was coming? She would be leaving. At one time that was all she had wanted, but that time had passed.

And yet, what if it said she wasn't coming? She would be forced to stay in the middle of nowhere, in a place that God took great delight in burying like a child with a toy car in a sandbox. This was her only chance to ever leave Barmy, Oklahoma.

Her hands trembled as she tore open the envelope. The message was short, Madame never wasted money on things like telegrams, the meaning clearly written in as few words as possible.

She had somehow finagled a way to get the train to stop in Barmy, Oklahoma, on Sunday, April 14, 1935, as it traveled through town. She estimated that time would be around two o'clock. Sugar was instructed to be waiting at the train tracks. The train would stop exactly five minutes and after that it would be gone, never to stop again. The trunk must stay behind in Barmy, but everything inside was worthless to her now.

She folded the telegram, placed it back inside the envelope, and buried it at the bottom of the trunk where no one could find it.

She glanced outside and saw Homer waiting there for her. It was a clear day; they could go for a walk.

"Hey Sugar," he said in that familiar way that melted her heart.

"Hello, Homer. Let's go for a long walk today . . . I think it will be clear."

To Homer it didn't matter. He was used to being out in the dust. He shrugged. "Okay. Where do you want to go?"

"Not to town," she answered him. "I have been there. Show me something that I have never seen."

They walked down the dirt road, away from the town, the cemeteries, the dump. The dust beneath their feet was smooth and slick to walk on; the fence along the side of the road was almost completely covered with a drift that had stopped there as if just for that purpose.

"Has it always been this dusty here?" Sugar asked.

"Naw. When I was little, it was real nice. This time of year there'd be wildflowers blooming in the fields, sorrel, Johnny jump-ups, violets, windflowers."

"When did the dust come?"

"When the rain stopped."

He always walked ahead of her, not by design, but because his legs were so much longer and it was his custom to move quickly. She ran to him and slipped her hand into his saying, "Slow down. Are we running a race?"

He laughed and pushed his hat back looking all around him. "I wish you could've seen this place when it was pretty. Maybe you'd like it better."

Her mouth opened, ready to tell him she'd be leaving on the fourteenth, but then it closed. She couldn't find the words. Instead, she merely, replied, "Maybe I would have."

His hand was warm, she liked the way hers felt inside of it, nestled safely, warm and surrounded. Impulsively, she leaned her head on his arm as they walked. She did seem to see the prairie with new eyes, perhaps because it was spring and hearts tend to be quicker to appreciate things after the long dull winter. Perhaps it was her company or perhaps it was because she knew she would soon be leaving. "You are right, Homer," she exclaimed after they had been walking a while. "This land is not flat."

Indeed, it did rise toward the west just as he had told her. A jackrabbit scurried by and a red-winged blackbird called to them from a fence post. The dust covered the tips of her shoes as she walked, it lay there innocently for now, but she knew at any time it could rise up and be borne away wreaking misery. But today, it seemed gentle, like the prairie itself. The wind was soothing, the sun not harsh, Homer was quiet, but he walked slowly, letting her take everything in, mindful of her short legs, and quick eyes.

They came to a break in the fence and he led her down into what was once a creek bed. There were a few small trees growing there, dust drifted beside them up to the lower branches. The creek was choked with it; it lay thick and deep in the bed. Sugar noticed with a slight chill, the truck owned by Etta Esmeralda's daddy still resting quietly nearby.

"I used to come here when I was little," Homer told her releasing her hand and walking along where the water once flowed, his eyes scanning the dust. "Sometimes I would find arrowheads. I reckon those will never be found again, so much dust lays on top of 'em."

Sugar sat down in the dust on the incline of the ground as it dropped toward the creek and watched him. He kicked at the dirt a little and looked around him and then sighed and his eyes went up to her. "I wished you could have been here, then."

She patted the ground beside her and he joined her, his lanky frame crumpling on the ground. He sat sideways, his gaze trained on her face and she looked out over the prairie, trying to imagine him, a little boy, running from his father, finding this creek, and taking refuge here.

As her eyes swept the dust, a tiny speck of blue caught her attention. "Homer, what is this?" she said rising and walking to it. She dropped to her knees and began scooping the dust away. A tiny blue flower emerged, as if by some miracle, a speck of color had accidentally been dropped on the tan, dusty landscape.

He knelt beside her. "That's a baby blue. They used to be everywhere."

"It's beautiful."

His eyes never left her face, a face transformed from its usual cynical expression to one of gentle wonder. "It is beautiful," he agreed but he was not talking about the flower.

Chapter Twenty-Three

Like many women in 1947, mama found herself pregnant. It was the beginning of the baby boom, the men were home from war and the natural by-product was babies, and lots of them. She was never a large woman, and each pregnancy she had seemed to be harder than the last. That pregnancy ended in the seventh month. The doctor said the baby simply got too big to live in mama's womb and we buried him at Grit Cemetery, very near to Pal Watson.

In 1949, mama found herself pregnant again and this pregnancy ended in much the same way as the one before it, except that she hemorrhaged, lost her womb, and almost lost her life. I was thirteen years old at the time and the whole episode made a huge impression on me. I remember peering into her room on those beautiful springtime days. She would have the shades drawn and would be crying in the darkness.

I cooked dinner every night for a month after the baby died. Daddy would come home from work tired and covered with grease. I can remember the look on his face, the apprehension in his eyes as he would come through the back door and set his metal lunch pail on the table. He would kiss me and make his way to the bedroom and the door would close. Generally, mama would join us for dinner and her eyes would linger on each of our faces.

After about six weeks, she stopped crying in her room. It was as if she woke up one morning and decided she may as well begin to live again, because she couldn't seem to die.

Daddy bought a radio and we would listen to the programs every afternoon, and on some nights there would be music. One Friday night in June, when the sun didn't seem to want to set, mama and daddy were on the front porch listening to the radio and I was inside with my little brothers. The door was open and there was a beautiful mellow breeze coming in freshening everything. I remember distinctly the song, *The Way You Look Tonight*, coming on the radio and a sudden movement on the porch caught my attention.

My brothers had all crowded at the window and were giggling and I joined them, surprised to see mama and daddy dancing in the yard. In a way, they did look comical. He was so tall she barely came to his shoulders. She was barefoot and her hair was down and he was in his old coveralls from work. I smacked all three of my brothers on the back of their heads and sent them to the backyard while I stood there watching mama and daddy sway together.

The tune ended and they continued to dance to a silent ballad, one I couldn't hear but they intuitively understood. It was, for them, a renewal of sorts, a reaffirmation that they would have one another, until the playing of that final coda. She had learned, long ago, how incomplete and feeble her song would have been without him.

In April of 1935, there were two women in Beulah's house of prayer discovering that life's melody isn't always the predictable tune you expect. Marigold struggled with her heart at night, pacing the floor while the baby restlessly kicked at her. She may not have been a brilliant person, but she had a profoundly good soul and definite ideas of right and wrong. Joe Brownfield was a question mark in her world of constants. Where she learned her romantic notions of marriage, no one could say but she believed a woman should be with only one man in her life. That being said, the truth of the matter was that few women in the 1930s had the luxury to remain single.

As Marigold lay awake at night pondering Joe's offer of marriage, a profound loss and longing filled her soul. She wished desperately that Joe could have been the first man she lay with, and when she thought this a deep sense of guilt would run through her for the child she was carrying. It was hard for her to reason away the two notions. She wanted the baby; she wanted it desperately, because Marigold must always have someone to love, and yet, she wished she had never been with the child's father. This was the crux of her dilemma, to want a child from a man she wished she had never slept with, and it hurt her because she felt she was being unfaithful to the father and unloving to his child.

When Joe came to visit, Marigold's heart would jump and her spirit would tremble, because she loved him and wanted him and didn't know if it was right. He was not well. She wanted to take him in her arms, and nurse him and take care of him, and her sense of morality would not allow her to. They seldom even touched each other; once he had kissed her on the top of the head and once she had held his hand, and yet their eyes were in constant communication. There was an unspoken understanding, a comprehension of one another that went far beyond words or touch.

Her late night mental wrestling made her tired and depressed and the weight of the child was uncomfortable and demanding. She knew it would be soon. The bloody show in the outhouse confirmed what she had already guessed at . . . all she could do was wait and wonder and try to reconcile her emotions and her mind.

Her misery was compounded by the dust and the bugs that seemed ever crawling in the shanty. Centipedes and ants, spiders of every size and grasshoppers were everywhere. She would sweep them out every morning with the dust, and every night they would come back, crawling in the bed sheets, in the food, across the tables.

Sugar's dilemma, while not as complex as Marigold's, was no less easy to bear. She wanted Homer, she wanted to stay with him, but she couldn't bear to be in a land where the grass never greened and the sky was seldom blue and the dust swirled around in a deadly cloud, waiting, stalking like a predator, killing with delight as many as it could. Those it couldn't kill outright with pneumonia, it killed in other ways. It killed with measles, appendicitis, and of course, suicide.

"Look at that, Marigold," Sugar said one afternoon peering from the window toward the Guppy house. Saucy Martin's Model A was, once again, parked outside.

Marigold joined Sugar and they looked at a little girl playing happily with Bing and Autry. "Is that Etta Esmerelda?" Marigold asked.

"Yes. It has to be," replied Sugar. They both stared in awe at the transformation. The little girl was clean and in a very fashionable dress. Her hair was cut short and bobbed, exactly like Saucy's, and she was laughing and chasing Autry while Bing stood by.

"She'll never know her daddy," Marigold said sadly.

Beulah joined them looking out the window. "Her poor daddy had to give her away. It ain't natural to live in a world where folks can't take care of their own."

Marigold was thoughtful. "But do you . . . do you think Saucy will love her as much as her own mother would have?"

Sugar brushed her aside. "Be reasonable, Marigold. Saucy has the means to give this child everything she needs . . . an education, food, clothes. Her parents were destitute."

"But," persisted Marigold. "Will she love her?"

Sugar rolled her eyes. "That is not important."

Beulah cocked her head to the side. "Not important?" She shook her head. "You was raised hard."

"Why?"

"Because all the pretty little things that Saucy gives her won't mean squat if she don't love her. A new dress is cold comfort when you is sick, or when you got the toothache, or when your heart is broke."

"And can she?" Marigold asked. "Can she love her as much as the boys?"

Beulah sat down heavily in her rocker. "Mr. Clinton had two children when we married. I loved 'em as much as any we had together."

"I never knew you had children," Sugar said with interest. She knew precious little about Beulah.

Beulah leaned back in the rocker and closed one eye saying, "I had eight. Watched every one of 'em die. They got malarial fever, tetanus, appendicitis." She sighed and told them, "Good Book says life is but a vapor that appears for a little while and vanishes away."

"Eight children?" Marigold said sinking into the chair beside Beulah. "How did you bear it?"

"How do you not? You got to move on, child."

"That is right," Sugar agreed. "No one dies from a broken heart."

Beulah fixed her eye on Sugar. "You right positive about that, girl?"

Sugar was surprised by the question. "Of course I am sure. How could they?"

"Etta Esmerelda's daddy died of a broken heart."

Sugar rolled her eyes. "Her daddy died of a gunshot wound, Mrs. Clinton."

"He died of a broken heart," Beulah retorted stubbornly.

Marigold knelt beside Beulah's chair and looked into her aged face. "And you loved Mr. Clinton's children, though they weren't yours?"

Beulah's weathered eyes smiled into Marigold's. "Yes, I did. After a while I just forgot they didn't come from my womb. They was as much a part of me as my own. I cried as much for them as I did for my own little ones. It is hard not to love a child."

Unexpectedly, tears smarted in Sugar's eyes. "If that is the case Mr. Guppy does a pretty good imitation of it," she said looking away.

"They's people in this world who never learn to love anybody but theirself. They's the ones who miss out in the end. The truth of the matter is, it ain't easy to love so's lots of folks never bother. Love requires sacrifice."

Sugar's ears perked up. "What did you say?"

"I said love requires sacrifice."

Her eyes went to the cross Homer had given her. Glancing up, she saw Beulah looking at her oddly, as if seeing inside of her skull. It annoyed Sugar and she abruptly slid the cross under the material of her dress, unable to look at it any longer.

Marigold glanced out the window at the little girl laughing in the sunshine. The child had no kin left on earth, but was mercilessly unaware of that distinction, joyful in the moment, in a way only children can be.

Chapter Twenty-Four

When I was about fourteen years old I decided to take daddy's old truck and see how far I could follow the train tracks. Mama and daddy had walked over to visit with Marigold and I knew I would have plenty of time, so I talked one little brother into working the clutch and brakes for me and the other two decided to go and watch the show.

We would have been fine except for just as we started for home, an old dog ran out on the road directly in front of me. I swerved to miss him and the next thing I knew we were all in the ditch and the truck had gone through someone's fence.

We sat there stunned after it had come to a stop and I climbed out slowly and looked at the damage. It wasn't bad, but the fence needed mending and the car had a dent that would be impossible to miss. It took a little maneuvering to drive back onto the road and by the time we started again, the sun was setting.

Daddy was always very dark skinned but on that day he was pale. I had never seen his face as ghost-like as it was when we met up with him as he walked the road looking for us. He didn't say a word about the dent or even ask us where we'd been. He simply ordered my brothers into the back of the truck and I scooted over in the seat as far as humanly possible, looking out the window and praying that my death would not be a painful one.

Daddy's face may have been pale, but mama's was red and flushed. She ran to the truck when we got home and helped my brothers out of the back, holding them tightly as they climbed down.

I'll never forget how angry she was that day. How could I do such a thing? I endangered my brothers' lives . . . worried her and daddy to death. What was in my mind?

The questions came at me in rapid succession and I was finally able to explain in a halting voice, my need to see where the tracks led. How far would I have to go to come to the end.

"You'd need something besides my old truck," daddy told me, and to my amazement, he began to laugh.

Mama was not amused. "And what do you find to be so funny, Homer Guppy?"

"She reminds me of you. You were always looking down the tracks when you were her age, remember?"

"But she scared us to death!"

Daddy agreed and said to me, very seriously, "Next time you want to see something, I'll take you. Don't go leaving without saying anything."

I didn't realize at the time, how close mama had come to leaving without a word.

In 1935 leaving was very much on her mind. It seems spring got distracted, so winter turned to summer. It was hot and every day the sun shone down cruelly through a haze of dust, happily breaking the soil that would soon be carried away by the wind. There was little respite from the dust and the yard was deep and thick with drifts. Everyone moved as if in a dream, or more likely, a nightmare, waiting for something: for the end of the dust and darkness. Waiting for life to begin again.

Mama was never able to bring herself to mention to daddy that she was leaving Barmy and decided to enjoy their final days together untainted by sadness. She was eager when she saw him and felt urgency, an apprehension because the end was at hand and she wanted to fill her days with him.

Her eyes lingered on his face, memorizing every line, every scar. She buried her nose deeply into his neck and breathed in his smell, trying to connect it with something in her memory so the scent would always bring him to mind. Her hands ran through his hair and down his back, she knew every bone, every muscle. She filled her mind with him so that when he was gone, she could bring him back, if only in her dreams.

She spent her final week obsessed with him, sneaking out every night the dust didn't fly. They would go into the barn with Eve and Mary and forget the starvation and hurt outside. Their eyes were only for each other. Lying on the straw, they would hold each other, feeling their hearts beating through their clothes and yearning for more.

She lay there on the last night, looking up at him as he leaned on his elbow. She reached up and touched his face, the whiskers on it rough against her hand. He took her hand and kissed it.

"I wish we could marry," he said out of the blue. It was spoken in the way someone says I wish I could fly, with no real hope of the dream's fruition.

There was something appealing about waking up with him every morning. She envisioned him as an older man, tall and strong, the hollows behind his shoulder blades filled out, the rib-cage no longer protruding. They would have a house, children, she would see to it nothing ever hurt him again. He began to cough and the reality of the dust and the dirt crept back into her mind.

"We're too young," she declared practically.

"I guess." It was a reluctant admission.

She ran her finger down his chin and Adam's apple. She was leaving the next day and should be happy, but her heart ached with a mighty hurt that seemed to want to suffocate her. He rolled over on his back and put his hands behind his head staring at the ceiling. "You know, for the first time in my life I want to get work, to do something besides hide from my dad."

She felt uneasy. "You could do anything you set your mind to."

"I was thinking I could learn a trade. Like maybe working on cars or something. What do you think?"

The question hurt Sugar because she knew he was thinking of her when he was making his plans. She felt like a coward, worse than Judas because she was betraying him with more than a single kiss.

She leaned up and looked into his face picking a piece of hay from his cheek. "Homer, I think if you want to work on cars you will be good at it."

"There's good money in it, too," he answered looking at her keenly evidently trying to get her to say more than she was willing.

She climbed on top of him and gazed down into his face desperately wanting to end the conversation he was so intent on having. It was a good distraction; he put his hand behind her neck and pulled her face to his, kissing her, holding her against him tightly, and making her want to be with him in a way she knew was wrong.

"Stop," she murmured into his ear as he kissed her neck.

He did and they lay there shuddering, desire welling out of every pore.

She finally rose and brushed the straw from her dress and walked toward the door, with him behind. It was a soft night, the moon was bright in a seldom seen clear sky and the stars looked like sprinkles of white sugar.

He stood directly behind her, his body pressed closed to hers, warm and comforting. "I remember when you used to be afraid out here at dark."

"I am not afraid anymore," she said. The revelation surprised her.

She felt his hand stroking her short hair. "Why?"

She turned to him. "Because you showed me the beauty of the sky at night." She laughed a little. "I guess I just didn't know what I was looking for."

"And you know now?" he said looking at her strangely. "You know what you're looking for?"

She turned away from him quickly, the cross around her neck feeling suddenly heavy. "Does anyone really know that?" she asked as a diversion.

"Yes," he said his face buried in her hair. He gathered her in his arms again. Tonight they were together; tomorrow would have to answer for itself.

Chapter Twenty-Five

A strange sound woke mama on Sunday, April 14, 1935. She lay there in bed wondering what it might be, when it occurred to her the song birds were singing. Then a loud bang startled her again. That was the sound.

She crept from her room and the first thing she saw was Beulah on her knees facing the window and praying in a strange language Sugar did not recognize. Beulah never stopped, she didn't even look up when Sugar entered the room, but continued on, her voice rising and then falling, an urgency in the strange utterances.

Marigold was in the kitchen, opening windows. Sugar realized the banging she heard was Marigold as she struggled to get the windows to break free of the dust.

As she entered the room, Marigold turned to her. "Ain't it a beautiful morning?"

To Sugar it was. This was the day she had waited for, the day she would finally put Barmy, Oklahoma, behind her. She went over and helped Marigold push the reluctant window open. A fresh breeze poured in on them, sweet smelling, warm and gentle. Marigold's nostrils flared as she breathed it in.

They turned around. The room was filthy, there were drifts of sand in the corners, the very walls were dusty. Marigold stretched and said in a contented voice, "Today, I clean."

It would be a long day. The train didn't come until two o'clock and Sugar decided cleaning would help her pass the time. She got a shovel from the shed, carefully averting her eyes from looking over at the Guppy household, and quickly came back inside. She scooped the dust into the shovel from the corners and took it out into the yard. Beulah's praying continued, unabated. It didn't stop when they offered her breakfast; it didn't stop when the front windows were opened, she didn't even stop praying at noontime when they offered her lunch. Sugar and Marigold looked at each other in surprise. It was as if Beulah was in some sort of trance. "I guess she'll eat when she's done," Marigold reasoned.

"What do you think it is she is doing?" Sugar asked.

"I don't know. She commenced it about three this morning. I ain't got a lick of sleep since then."

"Why not just ask her to stop?"

Marigold looked down. "Oh, I didn't want to disturb her."

"But she was disturbing you."

Marigold said nothing. "Marigold Lawford!" said Sugar in exasperation. "You have about as much spine as a night crawler."

Marigold's mouth turned downward. "That ain't it at all Sugar. I just figure why is my comfort more important than hers? Why should I get what I want?"

Sugar had been wiping the dust off the cupboard. She slammed the dishes back onto the shelf. "Well, why not?"

"Because sometimes you need to let others have their way. That's why."

"If you do not put yourself first, nobody else will. Look at you. You let your family use you as a bargaining chip like you were some kind of sow or milk cow. They sold you out, turned you into a whore and you stood there and let them do it! God almighty, Marigold, have you ever made a decision for yourself?"

Marigold was trembling as she faced Sugar. "Did you once stop to think that maybe I wanted to stay behind with Ensign? Did it ever cross your mind that my parents cried over leaving me and I told 'em to go. Well I did and I'd do it again. You don't know what it's like to be hungry. You've never laid in bed at night listening to your stomach rumbling and knowing they ain't nothing to put in it tomorrow either. Well, I have and I got tired of digging in the dust for my supper. I got tired of feeling sore and hungry all the time and knowing nothing was ever gonna change and things weren't never gonna get no better. I got tired of having nothing and if that makes me a whore then so be it. Ensign was kind to me. He only wanted what was his due as my husband and I gave it to him gladly 'cause I knew there'd be something to eat in the morning and I wouldn't have to dig in the dirt to get it."

"And what did all of Ensign's kindness get you? You are right back to where you began except now with another mouth to feed."

"That may be true, but I'll take care of myself like I always have. I may have been used, but I would never stoop so low as to use someone else."

Sugar squirmed before the pointed look Marigold was giving her. "What are you saying?"

"I'm saying you don't care about nobody but yourself and you never will. You're about the most coldhearted little hussy ever walked. I've seen out the window, what you do with Homer.

He worked and strained to find a stupid Mason jar that don't even exist and he follows you and loves you and what did it get him? You used him all winter and now that train is going to stop and you're going to be gone forever."

Sugar's heart flopped hard in her chest. "How do you know that?"

"You think you're so smart. Well, if you were you'd have figured out they ain't no secrets in a small town. Everyone knows it."

Sugar's throat tightened. "And Homer . . . does Homer know?"

Marigold looked at her hands and whispered, "Everyone knows."

Sugar felt like someone had punched her, she wheeled backward from the words as if they had been a physical blow. Homer knew she was leaving.

"Marigold," Sugar said in a choked voice. "Where is Homer?"

"I don't know." She looked at Sugar with a puzzled frown. "Why didn't you just tell him? Just leaving like that . . ." She shook her head. "I can't believe you weren't even going to say good-bye."

Sugar didn't want to explain it to Marigold. She didn't want to hear her voice say out loud that she was a coward, that she was weak. Instead, she asked, "When did he find out?"

"Yesterday."

Suddenly last night's conversation became clearer to her. The searching glances, the promises to find work. He was trying to get her to tell him what her plans were. He was giving her the chance to make it right and she never did. She wrung her hands. "I wanted to tell him. I meant to tell him." She sat down at the table and put her head on her arms. "He must feel so betrayed."

Marigold tried to comfort her. "Surely he knew you weren't going to stay here forever."

"But he never would have dreamed I would just disappear." Her heart froze as she thought of his mother and how she had hurt him. Now Sugar was doing the same thing, leaving without saying anything at all. It wasn't fair and it wasn't right. Suddenly Marigold's words from months ago rang in Sugar's ears: "If you hurt him, he could do something desperate." Sugar rose abruptly from the table. "I have to find him."

"Sugar, there ain't time. The train will be through in an hour."

"I can find him and still get to the station." She started to leave the house, and then paused, realizing she would never see Marigold again. A sudden feeling of affection came over her. "Marigold, I have to find Homer. I have to leave now." She looked into Marigold's face, a face she had grown used to seeing every day. It was unfailingly gentle and forgiving. She would miss her. "Thank you . . . for everything."

Marigold's eyes filled and she crossed the room and took Sugar in her arms. "You be happy, Sugar," she said in a hoarse whisper.

Sugar nodded and wiped her face with her hand. She rushed into the front room and was surprised to see Beulah gone. "Did you hear Mrs. Clinton leave?"

Marigold followed her and paused, surprised. "I'm sure I didn't." She glanced out the back window and returned saying, "Wagon's gone, too. That's the strangest thing."

Sugar started for the door and then turned around and took Marigold's hands. "Marigold, I want you to listen to me. That sheriff loves you and he will take you whether you can prove you were married to Ensign Lawford or not. That baby needs a daddy and he will give it a name."

"But it wouldn't be the baby's real name."

"Marigold, does that matter?"

"It does to me," she responded weakly.

"Then do something for yourself for once. Do not sit back and wait for Mr. Cope or Joe to take care of you. Go over there and get that license from Holcombe. If you are sure you were married, it has to be somewhere, right?"

"But, Joe told me . . ." Marigold began.

"Marigold, you are a grown woman, about to have a child. Are you not capable of doing anything for yourself? Just tell Holcombe you do not want his money. If he does have the license that would be the only reason he is hiding it. Then, you can marry the sheriff and everything will turn out."

"You're right, Sugar," Marigold remarked as if a realization came over her. "It all makes sense. Holcombe won't need the license anymore if I tell him I don't want the house or the money. Of course, he'd give it to me, then. There'd be no reason not to."

"It cannot hurt to ask," Sugar reasoned with her.

"Yes," Marigold said. "I just need to know once and for all. Maybe it's true that Ensign never married me. But, Holcombe was there. He could, at least, tell me the truth . . . then I'd finally know."

Sugar hugged Marigold. "Thank you for everything. Maybe after I get back to Chicago, I will write to find out how the baby is doing." A sudden tightening of her throat made it hard for Sugar to speak for a moment. "I will miss you, Marigold."

Marigold smiled her gentle smile. "We'll see each other again. I'm sure of it."

The two women parted, one to find her future the other to rectify her past.

Chapter Twenty-Six

My mama always said loving my daddy was like raising a baby bird . . . beautiful but oh so fragile. He always treated her as if she were infallible; any word from her was the gospel truth. I don't recall as a child her ever once raising her voice at him but if she were ever the slightest bit annoyed with him, his shoulders would slump, and his face would fall. It would break her heart and she would vow to never be impatient with him again. The truth of the matter was, he was hard for her to live with, but there wasn't another woman on earth who could. Mama learned that being god-like and all powerful like Madame Courtier had its disadvantages as well.

The gold cross jostled up and down as she ran to the street, looking both ways, hoping for a sign, some kind of mark to tell her which way to go. She saw nothing, so started for town first.

Everywhere she went, it was the same thing, "We hear you's leaving us today, Sugar," and "We sure gonna miss you around here, Sugar."

"Good Lord," she thought to herself in vexation, "how does everyone know?"

She ran into the drug store. "Mr. Wiley, you see Homer Guppy?"

Mr. Wiley paused in his shelf stocking. "He was in here about an hour ago. Looked a little upset, too."

"What did he say?"

He shrugged his shoulders. "Oh nothing really. Bought himself a Coke and just sat there drinking it and looking out the window."

Homer never had money; he had never even tasted a Coke. "Where did he get the money?"

"He put it on his daddy's tab and there'll be hell to pay for sure."

"Thank you," Sugar said shakily and walked back out into the spring day. Where could he be? Homer would never dream of putting anything on his daddy's tab; she couldn't imagine what was going on in his mind.

"Oh God," Sugar breathed in fear. Her heart felt cold and sharp in her chest. It pounded, loudly, quickly and she could hardly breathe for the fear that was rising up inside of her. She balled her hands and put them on her eyes, trying to will herself to think. Where would he have gone?

She ran next door to the dry goods store. It was closed for Sunday but she spotted Miss Pet behind the counter. "Miss Henson, you seen Homer?"

The pink head turned around at the sound of her voice. "Why Sugar," she said in her beautiful voice. "What a surprise. I thought you'd be at the train station."

Sugar was out of breath from running. She was hot from the warm April day and her legs were trembling from so much running. "Ma'am, I am trying to find Homer. Have you seen him?"

"Why, I guessed he'd be with you at the train station," Pet returned confused.

Sugar's eyes turned to the ground. "I never told him about the train," she confessed miserably. "I did not think he knew I was leaving."

Miss Pet's face grew white at this admission. "You never told him? And now he's gone?" She crossed the room and sank into a chair.

"What is wrong, Miss Henson?" Sugar asked in a voice filled with dread.

"It's just as I feared." Pet's face was sadly resigned.

Sugar sat before her. The train could wait. "Tell me what you are afraid of."

Miss Pet licked her lips and her eyes darted around the room as if she were afraid some kind of specter was listening, some malevolent spirit waiting for her to say the wrong thing. Finally, she began, "There's things about the Guppy household that this town just kind of buried away. Things folks don't speak of."

"What?"

Miss Pet took a deep breath. "When Linford Guppy was a young man he was quite handsome. He came back from the Philippines and folks treated him a bit like a hero. It all went to his head . . . he thought he was something. He decided he needed a wife to make everything complete and married Homer's mama. She was a pretty, young thing. Homer's mama grew up without a mother. Her mama had died bearing her and her daddy never got over it. They found him hanging in the barn one pretty day with his wheat all baled around him. Made a sizeable good income that year, but he weren't around to enjoy it. But Linford surely did."

"He married that child while she was still grieving over her daddy and he never treated her right. Things went on tolerably until he found out she was going to have Homer. He didn't want no baby taking his little wife's attentions away from him and he didn't like to spend any of his liquor money on the child."

"Truth be told, we think he poisoned her a few times trying to get her to miscarry, but it never worked. After nine agonizing months, Homer was born, puny, sickly, barely able to cry."

"Linford took to drinking even more to keep himself company. His desire for his wife paled in comparison to his desire for the bottle. When Homer was about one year old, Linford picked him up and threw him against the wall. Mrs. Guppy could stand it no longer; she couldn't protect Homer and it was killing her to watch him abused. She got away from Barmy the only way she knew how; she put a .38 in her mouth and pulled the trigger."

Sugar's stomach turned. "He never said anything . . ." she began.

"Oh, he don't know it," Miss Pet answered. "The whole town took to covering it all up. Our big shame, cause we couldn't protect her from her husband and we can't protect Homer now. Sheriff is the only one ever tried to do anything about it and Homer, well he wouldn't have it. Children can love the most worthless parents." She sighed. "All the misery of the world rests in a small town."

Sugar's heart began to pound with an awful realization. "Miss Pet, do you think Homer . . ."

"It's in the family. Homer always was more like his pretty little mama. Her daddy had named her Mourning 'cause his wife died with her and that set the whole thing in motion. Nothing but sorrow can come from it all."

Sugar rose quickly turning the chair over in her haste. "I have to find him," she said, panicked.

"The boy's a ghost," Pet said unhappily. "He's always been one able to disappear. Disappeared when he should have been in school, disappeared when his daddy was drunk and hollering. No one finds Homer unless he wants to be found."

Sugar was panicked. She wrung her hands in agitation. "And you do not know where he could be?"

Pet's eyes glistened with tears. "No, honey. I couldn't guess."

Sugar closed her eyes and took a deep breath. "I will find him. Thank you, Miss Pet."

She followed Sugar to the door. "What about the train?"

"I do not know," Sugar answered rubbing her face with her hands. She only knew that finding him was all that mattered.

Chapter Twenty-Seven

Marigold Lawford was an innately good person and every action was guided by this goodness. So good was she, in fact, that she was unable to conceive of the fact that not all people were like her. It had never crossed her mind that Holcombe would not do the right thing; in fact, she was never quite able to reconcile Holcombe's behavior on that Palm Sunday with her rosy notion of the world. When she spoke of it, she would simply shake her head and say, "But I'm sure the dear didn't mean it." But when I heard the story, and what he had done, I knew there could be no mistake. Holcombe Lawford had meant to do Marigold a harm.

As she rushed down the street, everything seemed clear to her. It was the first time in months she felt carefree and happy. The beautiful day added to her lightheartedness. In her innocent world, she would soon have the license in her hand and her baby would have his name.

She made her way to the Lawford estate and quickly moved up the walkway. She hadn't seen the house in eight months but it had not changed. It seemed as if it were frozen in time, waiting for her return. Rushing up the stairs, she knocked on the door. It was large and foreboding, blackened with time. Holcombe answered it and coolly regarded Marigold standing there.

"Hello, Marigold," he said acidly. There was no opening of the door, no welcome, just Holcombe's face peering out at her through the crack as if she were vermin, unwelcome and filthy. "My, how you've changed since the last time I saw you."

Marigold felt the damp sweat on her chest and back. She was suddenly nervous and her hands trembled. "Holcombe," she said her voice weak and shaking, "I know why you're doing this, why you're saying what you're saying, but you don't have to. You can keep all the money. I don't want it anymore; I just want the marriage license. I'm sure it must be here somewhere. If you give it to me, you can keep everything. That's not important to me anymore. I just don't want people saying my baby's a bastard."

Holcombe smiled a thin smile. "You must know I can't do that."

Marigold's hands dropped to her side helplessly, in surprise. "But why? You can have the money."

"Yes, but you'll have little Ensign with you and he could come claim his share of daddy's fortune at any time. I can't take that risk. I'm sorry."

"But he won't. I promise."

"You promise? Promises are merely delays before you do what you say you won't."

"That's not true."

"Oh, I think it is."

Marigold reeled. "But, this baby is your half-brother or sister. How can you be so cruel?"

"Marigold, do you have any idea how many half-brothers and sisters I have running around?" Holcombe smirked. "Every time one of daddy's little nannies got knocked up he'd give her a thousand dollars and a train ticket. He never saw fit to marry any of them. Why he married you I'll never know. Your family would have given you to him anyway."

"No, they wouldn't," Marigold argued. "And I wouldn't have stayed with him if we weren't married. I wasn't raised that way."

He coolly took a cigarette from its silver case, tapped it twice and lit it. "That was quite a virginal little speech. It almost took my breath away, it really did. Regardless of what any piece of paper says, you were never daddy's wife. You were never his equal in any way. You were his release at the end of the day, a soft, warm thing to roll around on. Property is all you were and if you weren't so big and unsightly, I'd take you as my inheritance."

"I was your daddy's equal," Marigold declared her eyes filling with tears. "He talked to me about everything, even you. He needed me because you didn't care about him and he knew it. But I cared about him, more than you could understand 'cause you're nothing but a heartless shell of a man, you've never been loved and you can't give what you never had."

Holcombe blew cigarette smoke into the air and watched it curl around. "I never had any use for daddy, other than his money, and that's a fact. He was a coarse, profligate son of a bitch and he embarrassed me every time he opened his mouth."

"He was a great man, Holcombe. He worked hard for everything he had; it wasn't handed to him like it was to you."

Holcombe leaned against the doorframe and crossed one foot over the other, regarding Marigold smugly. "Well, now he's gone and everything he worked for belongs to me and I intend to see it stays that way. There will be no license, and as I've told you before, the child will not lawfully be an heir. It was very easy to convince people that the wedding was a fraud, that daddy set the whole thing up to sleep with you. The license has been struck from the court abstracts by my friend, the judge. Now, Marigold, is there anything else I can help you with?"

Marigold wrung her hands in agitation. There is no help-lessness like that of the impoverished; she felt the door slamming shut. In desperation she cried, "Please, Holcombe, you'll ruin me. I'm a good woman; I come from a good family. Please . . . I'm begging you, give me the license." With that Marigold began to sob.

Holcombe dropped the cigarette to the porch and ground it out with his foot. "I grow bored with this. Good-bye."

Marigold saw the door closing and twenty-two years of mindless obedience raised its ugly head. Twenty-two years of "Yes, mama" and "Yes, Ensign." Her eyes began to burn and her heart raced. She threw her forearms against the door and shouted, "No!" with all her might, pounding on the door heavily with her fists.

Holcombe's mouth gaped open in shock. He did not antici-pate anything but mildness from Marigold and this outburst was unexpected. At that moment, Marigold saw in his eyes the only thing about Holcombe like his father. His eyes sparked with fury, she could see in his face his temper getting the better of him. She recognized the expression, the clenched jaw, the gritted teeth; she had seen it many times on Ensign's face, but Ensign would have never dreamed of directing his rage toward Marigold. He had always treated her with gentleness. Holcombe shook the door trying to get her to budge. "Let go. Get off my property this instant!"

"Not without the license."

"Get, now," he threatened, raising his hand above his head with a hatred that shocked Marigold with its ferocity.

"I won't," she answered defiantly, but flinching before the upraised hand.

That flinch was all Holcombe needed to see. It was, to him, an acknowledgment of his power over her. His hand crushed down on Marigold's face, stunning her with its force. She crumpled to the porch under its fury.

"Get the hell off my porch or I'll kill you!"

"No!" she sobbed on her knees looking at her hands. For a moment she marveled at how swollen they looked, and then wondered at the drop of blood that dripped there, in a thick bubble; warm, sticky and unmoving. Another bubble and then finally the weight of many bubbles caused the blood to run, in a thick red line.

"Stupid lousy bitch!" Holcombe shouted. He kicked her hard with his boot, and Marigold felt it crush into her hipbone, the kick driving her away from the threshold of his door. He slammed it shut leaving her lying on the porch.

She lay there stunned for a moment and quickly realized that a vague cramping feeling had come over her. Her water was broken and she was alone and helpless. Suddenly, she began to cry because there was only one face she longed to see . . . it wasn't Ensign's, though he should be there at the birth of his child. It wasn't even Beulah's, though she could help her through her labor. She needed Joe and her desire to see his face overwhelmed her and caused her to weep. And suddenly, he was there. He had seen the whole thing, the blow to her face, the door slamming shut. He had been running, as if in a dream, not able to reach her in time to help. But, he was there now and she felt an indescribable comfort in his presence.

His face was dark with anger. She could see his eyes quivering with a barely controlled rage. He scooped her up in his arms, and carried her, with some effort, to his squad car. The siren wailed, and the car pulled away.

Dewey Cope had also been running to help Marigold when Joe arrived. He had just returned from a successful trip to Oklahoma City and had gone to Beulah's to find her. Somehow, he knew where she'd be and he rushed over knowing what would happen. As soon as the squad car began to leave he directed his attention to Holcombe.

His fists were clenched, his temper had overwhelmed him and he was heading up the walkway fully intending to kill Holcombe Lawford when he spied Beulah's wagon coming. Dewey scooted up to the porch and hid in a corner of it, unwilling for her to see him.

As Dewey stood in the corner of the porch, he glanced inside and saw Holcombe standing in the middle of the room. He held in his hand the marriage license that Marigold had pleaded for. Holcombe lit another cigarette and watched the flame from the match with wild eyes. His moustache curled in an excited smile as he put the match to the bottom corner of the license and watched the blaze consume the paper. He threw the remains in the fireplace and then, sighing contentedly, put his hands in his pockets and opened the front door to enjoy the spring day.

He took a long draw on his cigarette and walked down the stairs with Dewey's burning eyes following him. He hesitated when he saw Beulah, but it was too late. She had already spied him. Pointing her finger at Holcombe, she said in a surprisingly loud voice, "The Good Book says, 'For affliction doesn't come forth from the dust but man is born to trouble as the sparks fly upward.' Holcombe Lawford, you just bought yourself trouble."

He stared after her as she drove off toward the highway in her wagon. A bird rushed by his head, startling him and causing him to jump. Another bird flew, fast and low; it brushed against him as it flew past. Then suddenly there were many birds flying around him, their wings beating against him, the sound of their frightened cries deafening. Jackrabbits and field mice came scurrying around his feet, making him stumble. Then Dewey heard a low rumble and his eyes followed where Holcombe was staring, as if in disbelief. A wall of thick, black dust was bearing down on Barmy at an amazing speed. It was rolling, boiling like a huge black wave, swallowing houses as if they were toys. They disappeared one by one and Holcombe stood too shocked to move as the mountain of dust thundered toward him. It was traveling fast, the hair on Dewey's arms and neck rose with the static electricity. He could see sparks, colored lights shooting through the darkness. Everything in its path was devoured in an avalanche of suffocating blackness. Holcombe ran for the house and got inside, and Dewey leaped from the porch and climbed underneath just as the storm slammed into town.

Chapter Twenty-Eight

Joe's face was pale and rigid; he sat silently, hunched over the steering wheel, leaning forward as if in hopes that this would urge the car to move faster. His hands gripped the wheel tightly; Marigold noted through her pain that the knuckles were surprisingly free of hair.

"Thank you," she managed to say weakly between contractions.

He turned to her, his hat pulled down so that she couldn't read his eyes. Finally, he said in a choked voice, "I thought I told you to steer clear of Holcombe." The voice was more frightened than angry. He began to cough violently and he buried his face in his sleeve.

"I thought I could reason with him. I figured if he knew I didn't want his money anymore he'd let me have the license. I never dreamed he was doing this from meanness. I just thought he was trying to keep what he thought was lawfully his."

"I hope you see what he really is," Joe told her with an edge of bitterness in his voice. "He struck you! By God I'll see him behind bars for that."

"Just let him go, Joe," Marigold begged. "The baby's coming and it don't matter no more. If it don't matter to you and you believe me, that's all that counts."

"You know I believe . . ." his voice trailed off. "Sweet Jesus," he breathed under his breath.

Marigold had been watching his face and she saw the change come over it. She tuned to the windshield and said lowly, "Oh my God." There was a cloud as black as night heading in their direction, it towered like a mountain, swirling, blowing toward them. Joe turned the car around and sped toward the jailhouse. They arrived with the storm.

"Come on!" Joe shouted grabbing Marigold's hand. Static electricity shocked them both and Marigold cried out in surprise. "Follow me," he told her quickly. Marigold scooted across the car seat and stopped in the middle of the road. The cloud was the most horrible thing she had ever seen, it seemed menacing, angry, like it wanted to bury her. "Hurry up!" Joe called.

She followed him into the jail and he slammed the door shut crying out in pain at the shock delivered by the door knob.

Marigold's face was white with fright. The inside of the jailhouse was dark but the metal bars were snapping with electricity, they glowed eerily, sparks popping off of them. "Is it the end of the world?" she asked in terror.

Joe lit the kerosene lantern. It flickered, casting shadows upon the walls, the light scarcely penetrating the blackness. "It's not the end of the world," he assured her.

They stood there in the stuffy, dim jailhouse and Marigold told him. "Joe, I'm about to have this baby."

He looked at her in disbelief for a moment and then his training took over. He moved to the back of the jail, threw open a closet and pulled out an inmate's uniform. "Put this shirt on," he instructed her. He only blushed a little when he added, "Don't put your under things back on."

She nodded and went to the little bathroom to change. She threw her clothes in the trash barrel. They were filthy and soiled and could not be saved. When she came out, he had pulled the cot in the cell from against the wall. There was a bucket at the end of it, a small washtub filled with water and a little stool on the side of the bed.

"I'm all set," he told her trying to sound encouraging.

She nodded but did not want to lie down just yet. "So this is where you spend your time," she said pacing around the dark jailhouse. The lantern on the desk flickered and she moved to it. Running her finger along the wooden top of the office chair she glanced at the desktop. It was Spartan with no pictures, no vase of flowers, nothing but a calendar and a notebook. It seemed a lonely place.

He was laying a pair of scissors and some sewing thread on the little nightstand in the jail cell. "Yes," he answered. "This is it. My home away from home." He took off his tan sheriff's shirt and hung it carefully on a nail. Marigold noted his dark skin ended at his shirt collar and wrists. She stifled a smile.

He came to the cell door and looked at her. "Everything is ready." He paused, "Are you scared?"

She crossed the room and stood before him in the inmate's shirt. She was so small it hung down below her knees. She shook her head. He took off his hat and ran his fingers through his hair. "Jesus, I am," he admitted.

At that moment, a huge pain engulfed Marigold. She reached for him and he supported her while she trembled from head to toe the intensity of the pain washing over her. Finally, she opened her eyes. Looking pale but composed, he helped her into bed.

As he sat beside her on the little stool, she unconsciously caressed his arm. "Joe," she said in a small voice. "I want Homer to come and live with us."

"What?"

"I think it would be better if he stayed with us. Don't you?"

Joe looked at her strangely. "Us? You mean you and me? Marigold, what are you saying?"

She looked into his face, more fully than she had ever allowed herself to look into it before. "I'm saying," she repeated, "when we get married I want Homer to stay with us. I know you worry about him and with Sugar gone, he'll need company."

His eyes smiled. "Okay. When are we going to have this wedding?"

A pain engulfed her and her brows knitted together. Afterward, she replied, "As soon as we can."

They sat there silently in the darkness while the storm raged outside. Her hand traveled down his arm to his elbow and her fingertips traced the ridges of it. "Why do I feel like I've known you all my life? You seem so . . . familiar."

"I don't know. But I know what you mean."

The storm slammed against the building with a wicked fury; you could hear the dust scouring across the stone front, across the windows; the wind howled loudly, thunder rolled. He stroked her arm. "We'll sure have something to tell this baby about when it's born," he said as the thunder and the dust rolled around them.

She smiled. "Is it okay, if I name him Ensign? After his daddy? It only seems fitting as Holcombe never had children. Seems the name should live on."

He stroked her cheek. "Ensign it is," he agreed. "Unless it's a girl."

Marigold looked surprised. "A girl?" she said in wonder. "I never even considered a girl."

"Why?"

"I don't know," she admitted. "It's just always been a boy to me."

Something crashed loudly against the jailhouse. Marigold jumped and then asked, "Do you think the train is okay?"

He couldn't answer for sure. "This storm is going a good fifty miles an hour. Likely, it caught the train, but don't worry. I'm sure they'll just stop it on the tracks and wait."

"I hope Sugar found Homer. She needed to say good-bye."

"He'll be fine. I'll go looking for him after the storm."

"Joe," she said quietly. "I think it's about time."

His face grew visibly paler, but he only responded, "Then, let's have this baby."

The dust pounded on the jailhouse, it bellowed and howled. But life must go on and no life is without storms. Ensign was born, strong and lusty like his father. He screamed angrily at the wind and Marigold comforted him with her breast.

Chapter Twenty-Nine

Sugar cursed herself as the world's biggest fool as she ran through town away from the train station, away from her ticket out of Barmy, Oklahoma. Her breath came in short, painful gasps but the fear in her would not allow her to stop running. Her side ached and she was sure she would vomit; the beautiful spring day's warm temperatures caused the sweat to stream down her back and chest. Her hair was wet with it, her face red and flushed, and yet, she would not stop.

She was on the other side of town when the train whistle blew. She stopped abruptly and turned toward the depot. She could see the smoke, she heard the bells ringing. The whistle blew again, calling her away from the dust and sickness. It seemed to be saying, "Sugar, your dreams are waiting. Come to me." And, yet, the vision of Homer somehow harming himself, of him being left alone and friendless was overwhelming. She sank to her knees, exhausted, panting for breath, sick and confused.

She imagined Madame's face if she showed up for the train now, filthy, disheveled, her clothes sticking to the sweat on her. The sharp nose would go up, the small glittering eyes would look down at her and she would point her to her seat without a word.

In Chicago, Madame would get her work, she knew. She would not have come for her if she didn't think she could use her, but the minute she was injured, the minute she put on too much weight, or she defied Madame, she would be out on the streets of Chicago, spit out like meat too raw or too overdone to be savored any longer. And then what? What work could a woman find in Chicago? She could be a telephone operator or shop girl, but there were one hundred applicants for each of those jobs. The thought of prostitution loomed before her mind. She had known at least a half dozen girls Madame had cast aside who had gone to work for Al Capone. The cruel reality was, there must be money to eat and the methods of earning it, limited.

She rose unsteadily to her feet, wobbling a little from exhaustion. She stood there wavering; she could stay in the dust or go home to the cold grayness of Depression era Chicago. The whistle blew again, sounding impatient like Madame herself. Sugar's face stung with the recollection of Madame's reprimands, the smacks for words spoken improperly, words spoken rashly, even words spoken in truth.

And, finally, her heart overruled her mind and her reasoning and fighting with it were at an end. She reached down and pulled off her shoes. "I am an idiot," she said to herself in exasperation, angrily flinging the shoes as far as she could. Finally, she heard the train pull away from the station, a last long whistle, accusing her of stupidity and foolishness.

She ran barefoot along the dust-covered road, searching, looking for any sign, any indication that Homer might have come this way, and suddenly, like a gift from God, one long footstep appeared in the dust, followed by another and another. Long feet, long stride, it had to be him.

She followed the footprints. They took her out of town, past the cemetery and toward the creek bed, Homer's place of refuge. She followed the road until she reached the opening in the fence, almost afraid of what she would find. She saw the truck near which Etta Esmerelda's father had shot himself. Could it be possible that the truck had seen another man die? And then suddenly, to her relief, she saw Homer standing, his shoulders slumped, his hands in his pockets, watching the train as it picked up speed and traveled westward out of town.

She could hardly find her voice she was so overjoyed. Finally, she could contain herself no longer. "Homer!" she cried bounding toward him, dirty, exhausted and out of breath.

He turned in surprise and she leaped on him, legs around his waist, hugging him tightly, covering him with kisses. She looked into his face and was surprised to see that he had been crying.

He put her down and stared at her in amazement. "Where'd you come from? I heard the train."

She put her arms out to her sides. "I could not go."

"What do you mean you couldn't go?"

"You must know what I mean."

"You mean you stayed . . . because of me?"

"There is no accounting for taste, Homer Guppy, but I think I must love you."

He put his hands in his pockets and cocked his head to the side, staring at her as if he couldn't comprehend her, as if she were beyond his understanding. A look of profound relief and comfort shone through his eyes and his slow, crooked smile began forming on his mouth.

He couldn't help but say a little worriedly, "You may regret this, Sugar."

Her arms slid around his waist. "I know that. But there was nothing I could do. I tried to fight it but in the end, Barmy turned out to have more to offer than Chicago."

He buried his face in her filthy, snarled hair and she felt his breath on her scalp. It was comforting, it was the breath of life, the proof that she had saved him, and in turn, had saved herself.

She stood there trying to catch her breath when Homer raised his head abruptly. At that moment, a jackrabbit ran between her legs, almost knocking her over. Homer looked around, his face wearing a look of disbelief. Sugar glanced up; all around were hundreds of jackrabbits, fleeing as if from a predator, hopping all around them, running away from something.

"I don't like the feel of this," Homer began. "We'd better . . ." At that moment, he grabbed her hand and a numbing, hot sensation tingled up her arm. The shock knocked Sugar off her feet. "What the hell?" he said in amazement shaking his hand while she picked herself up dazed and confused.

He looked up and his eyes grew wide. "We've got to move," he told Sugar in a rush and Sugar turned to see a tumbling mass of dust racing toward them. The sky was eerie and green, the air static and charged with electricity.

He took his handkerchief and tied it around his hand. "Here," he said tying the other end around Sugar's wrist. "We've got to get to the truck." It was unearthly; the whole world had grown silent before this storm, as if it were trying to hide from the scraping menace that sped toward them. There was no wind, no sound, just the horrible sight of the black cloud.

The idea that this could be the end of her, that she had stayed behind for nothing crowded into her mind. "Then this is how it will be," she thought frightened beyond the capacity of any emotion. She had done what was right, she had come back to Homer and she knew she would rather die than live like a coward, afraid to love, afraid to suffer for it. "Love requires sacrifice," she mumbled to herself.

The storm moved so fast, it hit before they reached the truck. It knocked them both over with its fury pressing them into the ground. Sugar's eyes, ears, nose, and mouth quickly filled with dust. She couldn't see, couldn't hear, couldn't breathe. "This is what death feels like," she thought to herself as she lay on the ground unable to move, unable to even discern if she were face up or face down because of the swirling madness around her.

What felt like hours to Sugar, in reality, had only been seconds. Homer was pulling her along painfully. She was dizzy, disoriented, she wanted to stay put and die, but he persistently yanked at her arm. Suddenly his face was near her ear. "We can't stay here," he shouted over the wind. "We need to move. We're almost there."

Sugar doggedly crawled behind him, choking and gasping for air. Sight was impossible, her eyes were caked shut with mud, she panicked wishing desperately for oxygen. She pulled hard on the handkerchief and suddenly Homer was beside her. "I cannot breathe," she told him.

"Just a little further," he reassured her.

She fought hard against the panic welling up within her. It was like drowning, she could get no air into her lungs. She wanted to scream but she couldn't with all of the sand swirling around. All she could do was crawl after Homer, step after agonizing step. She knew her knees were cut and bleeding but her mind couldn't register pain, only shock.

Finally, she sensed the truck in front of her, solid and unmoving, a constant in a swirling world of sand. She heard the door being flung open and then she was lifted up and thrown inside. A door was slammed shut and then the wind was gone.

"I can't see," she said her voice trembling in the darkness.

His arms went around her, comforting her. She could feel the warmth of him, she could hear his breathing, the silence was so profound, she could hear her heart beating, the blood was pulsating in her ears. She coughed, her lungs painfully begging for oxygen. Dust was coming up from them, dust and spittle and mud. And the darkness was terrifying. Her eyes were open and were seeing nothing and her brain was disoriented, it felt as if the air were bearing down on her thick and black like death.

"You're shaking," Homer whispered into her ear. She moved closer to him. He was solid and tangible, he was the only thing in her world that was concrete and she had almost lost him. Her heart began to pound loudly, painfully. She needed him, she wanted him. She wanted to be with him and she didn't care if it was wrong . . . she was frightened, confused, hungry, and would not be denied.

She could not see anything, but she could feel him. Her hands moved up his chest to his face and she pulled it down and began to kiss him, greedily. He pulled back from her a little, but she was persistent. She needed to feel his skin next to hers; she needed to feel that she was not the only human being in the dim nightmare that was this reality.

She unbuttoned his shirt and then slipped off her dress and they lay there together, feeling the warmth of their skin as it touched for the first time. They fumbled in the blackness, ignorant of what they were doing. She knew nothing of men and could not see his face, she didn't understand why he cried out in the darkness, and why his head dropped next to hers, his breathing labored, his body spent and exhausted. But she did understand a choice had been made and that she must now forever stay in Barmy.

And the cross and the medal had become tangled in her hair and she left them there, unwilling to move. Homer's face was close to hers. She could feel his breathing as it slowed and became regular and she realized that he had drifted off to sleep. The sound of his breath was like a shield keeping the darkness from crushing the life out of her.

She began to shake because of the decision that she had made. But Homer was real and she realized that he was the only real thing she had ever known. Her arms went around his neck, she pressed against him and then she, too, drifted off to sleep as the storm screamed outside.

Chapter Thirty

The storm had not quite passed when Dewey came thundering into the jailhouse, his face red and his eyes glowing with excitement. "The Lawford Estate is burning!" he bellowed, startling Marigold who was gazing at the face of her infant.

Joe jumped up and grabbed his shirt, putting it on quickly. He rushed past Dewey who was staring at the child, his eyes moist, his mouth slightly open. "Is that the little one?" he said in a voice of reverence. They soon heard the squad car start and the gravel kick up under the spinning tires as it raced toward the estate.

Dewey moved across the room and gazed at the child. Marigold smiled up at him. "This is Ensign Lawford, Junior," she told him. "That is his name whether the law will acknowledge it or not."

Dewey sat down on Joe's office chair and rolled it to the door of the cell. "It will be acknowledged all right," he told her. "I've seen a friend of Ensign's in Oklahoma City. A certain judge he has been corresponding with. There will be hell to pay at the Beaver County courthouse tomorrow."

The baby yawned widely and Dewey and Marigold both laughed. She looked up at him. "Do you want to tell me what has happened?"

Dewey leaned back in the chair. "I always thought I knew what Ensign was up to." He shook his head. "I reckon I didn't know everything. In twenty-nine, Ensign took a pretty good hit to his investments. He pulled everything out of the stock market and chose to invest more in his own endeavors, those being wheat and real estate. Unfortunately those two items are next to worthless in Oklahoma and his annual income dropped to almost nothing in 1932.

"A friend of his, an accountant in the city of St. Louis, contacted him about some business dealings he had heard about. It was a sure deal, a way for Ensign to inflate his income, so he trusted this friend and gave him a sizeable amount of money for investing. His friend rewarded this trust, by buying stock, selling this same stock and doubling the amount within three months.

"Behind my back, Ensign had developed a habit. In the course of the next two years Ensign and this businessman worked together a lot. The man would telegram Ensign, Ensign would draft a check, and he would receive a much larger check several months later after the stock had been sold.

"It seems Ensign got a letter from a Mr. Joseph Kennedy in July of 1934. Mr. Kennedy is the head of the Securities Exchange Commission and his letter informed Ensign that he was in violation of the new Securities Exchange Act.

"Knowing my friend, I'm sure it came as a shock. I believe the shame of being caught in a scheme, or, more than likely, the shame of being found ignorant of knowing that what he was doing was wrong almost broke him.

"Being a right-minded individual, he was in the midst of figuring who was owed what when he died. When Holcombe asked me to fill out his federal tax form, he couldn't have known that what I would find would be your golden ticket. Stuffed in his receipt book, in a place lazy Holcombe would never dream of looking I found a letter Ensign was in the middle of writing. According to this letter, he intended to turn over his ill gotten gains to the U.S. Government and take whatever punishment deemed appropriate, whether it was a fine or jail time.

"He specifically states that neither his son, Holcombe Lawford, nor his wife, Marigold Lawford, had any knowledge of the nature of his business dealings, thus saving you from the nasty business of having to deal with the U.S. Government.

"The letter, coupled with the last three years of jointly filed federal income tax forms is enough, according to the judge in Oklahoma City, to prove that you and Ensign was married."

Marigold's face was flushed and her eyes were glowing. "So, we were married?" she asked timidly afraid she had misunderstood Dewey.

"Yes, ma'am. In every sense of the word."

Marigold closed her eyes and one tear slid beneath the lashes and down her cheek. "I knew he wouldn't do me like that. I knew Ensign wouldn't lie." She opened her eyes and saw Dewey looking at her kindly.

"You really loved him, didn't you?"

Marigold nodded. "Mr. Cope," she said quietly. "I am planning to marry again. Do you think it wrong of me?"

Dewey rose and crossed the room to her glancing down at the infant. He patted her shoulder. "I think Joe is a lucky son of a bitch," he told her and turned moving toward the door. Pausing he turned back. "Mrs. Lawford, I think it's what Ensign would have wanted."

The storm had finally died down and the world had not come to an end.

Chapter Thirty-One

Sugar woke with a start and sat up quickly. It was dark outside, but it was not the crushing blackness of the storm. She could see the stars, they twinkled down peacefully, making her wonder if it had all been a dream.

Her eyes went to Homer, still sleeping soundly in the most uncomfortable position she could imagine, something he seemed to be used to. Her eyes traveled down his body. She had never seen anyone so thin. His ribcage protruded out, not only in the front but also the sides of his body, even his shoulder blades were prominent. This was what she had traded Chicago for, a skinny boy with no future. No wonder Madame was so strict with her and wouldn't let her speak with whomever she pleased. Maybe the woman knew she had this tendency toward being attracted to what was beneath her. She must have realized that Sugar would be just like her mother.

And suddenly, Marie's marriage to her father didn't seem quite as preposterous as Madame had always made out. Marie had found love and that very love had caused her to be fearful because it was so great and wonderful that she was afraid to lose it. In a way, Sugar realized that Madame was right; her father had contributed to her mother's death. But it wasn't because he distracted her, but because he caused her to want to hold on too tightly. The fear of losing that which she found most lovely ended up being the thing that took her life.

She was trying to untangle the medal and cross from her hair when she woke Homer. He seemed disoriented at first, not remembering where he was and then his eyes fell upon her. "Let me help you with that," he said sitting up. He pulled the strands of the hair from the chains and then untangled them from one another.

They sat there for a moment in the truck, neither of them clothed, but feeling no shame or embarrassment. Her head was leaning against his chest; she was listening to his heart beat, when he asked her, "Are you okay?" The question meant so many things.

She looked up into his face. "Am I okay?" she repeated. She had lost her ticket to Chicago, her virginity, even her shoes. Finally, she responded, "Yes. I think I am okay."

"If you need to get back to Chicago, I'm sure we could try to get the train to stop again."

"No. I really think I will be alright."

His eyes lingered on her face. "I'll take care of you."

"I know."

They began to dress, and he told her, "We might want to think about getting married . . . just in case."

She remembered him in the blackness and felt a faint blush on her cheeks. "Yes, you are right."

The door of the truck didn't want to open, the weight of the dust against it made it heavy. Finally, he leaned against her a little and kicked it with all his might. The dust flew and the door swung open. Climbing out, they squinted in the darkness at the creek bed. It was nearly even with the land surrounding it, the truck almost completely buried, the trees mostly submerged.

"The baby blue," Sugar said mournfully.

"There'll be more," Homer promised her. They walked back to town hand in hand, looking for Beulah.

They got to Grit Avenue and Sugar's heart froze. The roof had been blown off the shanty, and one of the walls had come down. "Beulah?" Sugar called afraid the woman was hurt inside of the collapsed building.

She and Homer ran to the house and he flung open the door that was hanging on only one hinge. He lit the kerosene lantern and they looked around them. The house was submerged in dust, it lay thickly on the stove, the floor, all the tables and chairs.

"Beulah?" Sugar called into the darkness. She opened the doors to each of the tiny bedrooms, peering into them and finding each as devastated by the storm as the other. "She is not here," she told Homer.

He was standing in the part of the house that was the kitchen, holding the lantern, and he had an odd look on his face. "Look," he told Sugar.

In the middle of the table, surrounded by dust, but clean and sparkling stood a large Mason jar. They both walked toward it, slowly as if in a dream. "Where do you suppose it came from?" Sugar asked in awe. It had not been there during the storm that was obvious.

He touched it, gingerly, almost as if he were afraid of it. Clearing the dust from a place on the table, he sat the lantern down beside it and unscrewed the lid. Inside of it were wads and wads of cash. Their eyes met in shock.

"What is that?" Sugar asked him noticing a piece of paper beneath the jar.

He picked it up. It was a piece of paper on which were simply written the words, "FOR THE GUPPYS."

Sugar sank onto a chair, dumbfounded, and she felt the miraculous medal slip from around her neck and fall into the dust. And she was too shocked to move or care. Homer dropped to the ground beside her, leaned his head against her, and they sat there unspeaking, unable to comprehend or think.

Chapter Thirty-Two

I was born on January 12, 1936, on a ragged, wasted little strip of land known as the Oklahoma Panhandle, almost nine months exactly after the day that came to be known as Black Sunday.

The day Ensign Lawford, Jr. was born was the day his brother, Holcombe died. His charred body was found in the remains of the old Lawford Estate and no one in town mourned him except for Marigold. It seems the fire that burned the house started in the fireplace. Evidently, there had been something smoldering there and the wind whipped it up enough to send sparks flying throughout the house. Dewey Cope swears it was the marriage license, but I reckon no one will ever know for sure.

Holcombe had spent his last days working to secure for himself money that wasn't even there. It seems after the Securities and Exchange Commission was through, Ensign was, for all purposes, broke. Marigold always said it was a grace that Holcombe didn't live long enough to find that out.

She and Joe drove over to Cimarron County three days after the storm and were married, proudly displaying a marriage license bearing the names of Joe Brownfield and Mrs. Marigold Lawford, with the emphasis on the missus.

Marigold gave the land the Lawford Estate stood on to the state of Oklahoma with the stipulation that they build a penitentiary there. Construction was completed in 1939 and most people in town found work there.

Mama desperately wanted to see Beulah again. She had so much to thank her for and she really wanted her to preach at her wedding. The town searched day and night for Beulah, but after three weeks, it became evident that mama and daddy couldn't wait any longer. I was born exactly seven months, three weeks after they married and they named me Mourning Guppy, proving to the world that happiness can come from Mourning and good from a Guppy. They bought a house on the other side of town and Linford Guppy died two weeks after I was born. He never saw me.

Every year as far back as I can remember, my daddy took the family to the circus in Oklahoma City. It was a holy pilgrimage of sorts; the big tent was our Mecca, P. T. Barnum our prophet. Not until years later when mama was in one of her rare talking moods, did I understand why daddy scrimped and saved for that trip every year. She had stayed behind for him, she had given up the only life she had ever known and it was his way of giving a little bit of that life back. To him, it was an offering of love.

Mama never regretted not going back to Chicago with Madame Courtier, although sometimes I would see her take out her little raspberry-colored satin circus outfit and try it on. Daddy says he fell in love with mama the first time he saw her in it and I blame it for at least two of my baby brothers.

I'd be lying if I said life was always easy for them. They lost two children to the dust and daddy was never quite the same after the war. Still, I know mama never doubted in her heart that she had made the right choice. After all, she knew love required sacrifice. Instead of going back to Chicago, she remained here to love my daddy with the most fierce, protective love I have ever witnessed and she learned to find beauty in a wasteland.

I can remember sitting outside one night on a blanket with mama while daddy was away at war. It was summertime and the heat in the house was unbearable. My brothers were sleeping and mama was gazing at the sky. Pointing upward she said, "Mourning, that is the dog star." Daddy had taught her about the stars, he had taught her to not fear the dark, he had taught her how to soar.

So I was finally able to put together the events that brought Sugar Watson to Barmy, Oklahoma, and set in motion this thing that is my life. The only disappointing thing to me is I never got to meet Mrs. Beulah Clinton. You see, I am her namesake, in a way, and being brought up with the name Mourning Beulah Guppy was not an easy thing I can tell you. But I could never find out anything about her. No one knew where she went on that Black Sunday, no one ever heard from her again. Dewey Cope was the last person to see her and he could only point me in the general direction in which she rode off.

I was finally able to get to the library at the University of Oklahoma in Edmond one Thursday afternoon. After looking in numerous books, I, at last, came across a biography about her. She was just the way mama described her to me. The funny thing was, according to the book, she died when the jailhouse burned down in Piney Bluff, Arkansas, at the height of the Piney Bluff church wars. That was in the year 1921. I haven't really mentioned this fact to mama. I probably never will.

About the Author

Cynthia A. Graham is the winner of several writing awards, including a Gold IPPY and a Midwest Book Award for *Beneath Still Waters*, and her short stories have appeared in both university and national literary publications. She attained a B.A. in English from the Pierre Laclede Honors College at the University of Missouri in St. Louis. Cynthia is a member of the Historical Novel Society, the St. Louis Writers' Guild, the Missouri Writers' Guild, and Sisters in Crime. She is the author of two works of historical mystery: *Beneath Still Waters* and *Behind Every Door. Beulah's House of Prayer* is her first foray in the land of magical realism.

CPSIA information can be obtained
at www.ICGtesting.com
Printed in the USA
LVOW12s1454110716
495864LV00003B/33/P